The Cat of Small Town

DEDICATION

To my wonderful little sister, Aria, who inspired me to keep writing every day, and to my parents, who supported me greatly – I.T.

For my best friends, Ira, Kathleen, Chris, and Ahmet -Z.Ö.

The Cat of Small Town

The Cat of Small Town

Ira Thackeray & Zeynep Sena Özkan

The Cat of Small Town

Copyright © 2023 Tree of Life Stories LLC

Treeoflifestories1@gmail.com

Ira Thackeray, Zeynep Sena Özkan

All rights reserved.

ISBN 9798870719245

The Cat of Small Town

CONTENTS

Prologue	Pg #2-6
Chapter 1	Pg #7-14
Chapter 2	Pg #15-29
Chapter 3	Pg #30-36
Chapter 4	Pg #37-52
Chapter 5	Pg #53-74
Chapter 6	Pg #75-78
Chapter 7	Pg #79-88
Chapter 8	Pg #89-98
Chapter 9	Pg #99-106
Chapter 10	Pg #107- 128
Chapter 11	Pg #129-138
Chapter 12	Pg #139- 157
Chapter 13	Pg #158-168
Chapter 14	Pg #169- 174
About the Authors	Pg #176
Image keys	Pg#177-179

The Cat of Small Town

The Cat of Small Town

ACKNOWLEDGEMENTS

We are very thankful to:

The Supreme Power for bringing this book to life, and for our ideas and resources

Tree of Life Stories LLC for having faith and trust in our story

Our teachers, parents, and friends for always being so supportive and encouraging`

Ira and Zeynep

-Prologue-
2 Months Ago

I was too "young" at that time to understand what happened. Hazel and I were playing by the river on the rocky shore, feeling the miniscule shells crunch under our feet as we hopped around. Usually, my friends and I called it the "Claw River" since it had spiked rocks that looked like a huge monster was going to pounce on us any moment. There were also many other kinds of rock that twinkled like the stars at night. I particularly liked those ones.

Hazel and I were skipping rocks across the river to see whose rock would travel the farthest.

I counted every skip under my breath. "One...two...four...seven...eleven..."

My rock lost momentum and I watched as the clear water swallowed it up and it sank out of sight.

Hazel picked up a smooth pebble and hurled it across the water. It successfully made it 28 skips before her rock sank as well.

"Aww man!" I complained. "You're too good, Hazel. I think this game is rigged."

"It's not, Penny!" Hazel elbowed me, and her curly chipmunk tail curled around mine. "You act like it's the end of the world!"

Her nickname for me was "Penny". I didn't quite know if I liked it or not.

Suddenly, my hair stood on end. The air felt different and big waves crashed onto the shore. Our rocks were swallowed by the huge walls of water, and we couldn't even play anymore. As the wind howled, the blood rushed to my ears, and the harsh breeze started to come at us. I felt my dress being pulled with the wind. Hazel and I exchanged glances at each other and thought the same thing.

We had to run. Run away from the river and pass the erupting volcano, which was called Mount Anaconda, and back to our shelters...our homes. I ran while rocks crushed under my black loafers. The wind pushed me back like it wanted to stop me from running. The air smelled like smoke and burned flesh. The dark gas filled up my lungs and all I could do was cough, but I kept going. My tail was unhelpful, as it kept on pushing me behind with the wind. Before I realized Hazel was nowhere to be seen, I was out of breath. Too scared to even scream for help. I coughed and coughed because of the smoky air. Then I felt the ground shake under my feet. I tried to turn my head to look at my surroundings, but a loud sound...the loudest I had ever heard came from behind me.

    I screamed at the top of my lungs as I was suddenly thrown up into the sky. As I flew up into the smoke, I stared down at Animalia in terror. All I could see was smog and lava. There were vermillion reds mixed with the flaming lava, and dark gray and black spots dotted my vision. Every place in the town I cherished and loved, even the dainty little house I lived in, was destroyed. All I could think was, *Is my family okay?*

    Before I could do or say anything, I began to fall. I was too frightened to even remember the variable called gravity. As I fell, my longish dark hair covered my face from seeing my horrid surroundings.

Then I heard the fluttering sounds of gentle wings. I closed my eyes, and I landed in the soft and kind arms of someone. As I was quite dazed, I didn't know what had happened, but I heard someone shout, "Penelope!"

The voice echoed in my mind. *Am I dreaming?* My eyes opened slowly. All I could see was fire and a pointy nose looking down at me. *A nose shaped like that?* As my vision cleared, I saw the speckled brown wings I heard flapping earlier.

"Penelope! Are you okay?" asked the person.

I looked around me, I was laying down on the soft green grass. I sat up slowly, and I scanned my surroundings carefully. I looked at my savior, even though I knew I could have landed on my feet. It was my older sister, Clara.

My sister was a half sparrow and half human, a bird Animalian. She had beautiful blue shining eyes, long blonde hair like Mom, and her dotted wings made her stand out among the crowd. She could soar into the sky like a free bird at any time. I

The Cat of Small Town

wished I could fly, but I knew I was grateful that I was half cat and half human. I would never trade my flexibility or speed.

"Wh-where's Mom and D-Daddy? Wh-where's home?" I stuttered.

Clara was silent for a few moments, staring down at her bright shoes, which were now covered in soot and ash. "They're safe, Penelope. I-I think I flew over them. B-but is your head alright? When I carried you down, some of your hair singed off..."

I patted my scalp. It was spiky, stiff, full of soot and ashes, and I hated how it felt.

Clara knelt next to me and spread her arms. Her eyes were full of tears, and I'd never seen her cry before. I cried into her shoulder as I realized Mount Anaconda had erupted and had destroyed everything I knew and loved.

-Present-
CHAPTER 1

I was shaken awake. Clara was by my side in the backseat of our small station wagon.

"Are we here?" I asked.

"Almost," Clara replied. "I just woke you up for the fun of it, to be honest."

I rolled my eyes and leaned forward into the front seat. I watched my mom's fluffy fox tail swish back and forth as the car bumped down the tunnel.

"Mom?"

"Yes, honey?" my mother replied, turning in her seat to look back at me.

"How far away are we?"

"Oh, we're not very far from Small Town. Once we get past the tunnel, just a half hour drive, and we'll be there!" she smiled.

"Wait," Clara cut in. "Did you just say, 'Small Town'? Is that where we're going to live? It sounds dumb. Like, why would anyone name their small town, 'Small Town'?"

Our parents exchanged glances, but Mom turned to Clara and gave her one of her famous warm smiles. She didn't say anything, but Clara seemed to understand her mistake and looked down at her feet for a few moments.

Then her head snapped back up and she asked, "Hey Dad, didn't you go to college in Humania?"

Dad's bison horns turned to the side as he glanced momentarily at us. "That's true, Clara. I came here after I won a scholarship, and how could I refuse? Humania has much better technology, and education was a top priority in our family. So, I stayed there for at least three years when, during winter break, my parents called me to come visit them back in Animalia. That's when I bumped into..."

Mom chuckled.

"Your mother," Dad continued. "We kept in touch, and after I graduated, we got married and settled down back in Animalia. We wanted our children to be in touch with their roots in nature. I never thought we'd end up here..."

Mom suddenly elbowed Dad and gave him a look I'd never seen on her face before.

My cat ears twitched slightly as Clara scowled. "Would you guys *stop* keeping secrets from us? We know you don't want to bring back the memories of Mount Anaconda erupting, but the past is in the past. *No* going back, no matter what! You don't have to "protect" us," she did finger quotes.

Mom and Dad fell silent. So did I. I considered myself mature ever since the volcano erupted, and when I was "young", I was bright and bubbly. But now I had grown quieter and less sociable.

I fingered my short black, messy hair and stared out the moonroof of our station wagon with my violet eyes. I saw sea life floating above the underwater tunnel we were traversing through into Humania, where all the humans who had no magic or animal traits whatsoever, or so I thought, lived.

A huge whale with her calf swam over the tunnel, and they seemed to fly underwater majestically. I held my breath until they passed by.

"Clara!" I pointed to it as it was in the corner of my vision. "Did you see that whale with her kid? It was amazing!"

Clara didn't respond. I cocked my head and realized she was half asleep. I reached behind me and grabbed a spare blanket from our trunk, not like there were many belongings inside. I threw it over her and made sure her wings were tucked in comfortably.

"Goodnight," I whispered. Then I threw a side of the blanket over myself and dozed off.

***

"Penelope," Mom patted my shoulder, and I rubbed my eyes. "We're here."

"W-We are?" My voice shook at the thought that I had arrived at my new home.

I quickly jumped up from the seat and opened the car's door as fast as I could. We all hustled outside, and a small but homely cottage greeted us.

Mom walked up to me. "Well, this is our new home! Thank God we had enough money to buy this lovely house."

"Woah! It looks like it's from a fairy tale," I said.

I scanned the house. It had flowers and overgrown vines on some of the walls, but it still looked fantastic with all the greenery. A small but not too small, cracked water fountain stood next to a weeping willow that sat close to one of the windows of my new house. As I ran to the dark green front door, the grass crunched under my feet just like it used to in Animalia.

"Mom...I miss home," I said in a low, sad voice when I stepped onto the threshold.

I looked up at my mom's face.

Her blonde hair and white ears waved in the wind. I judged her face and immediately realized I shouldn't have said anything. She was pale, and I was afraid she'd faint any moment. She grabbed the neck of her white blouse, trying to stop herself from crying.

"Well...t-to be honest...I miss i-it too, Penelope, but this is a new beginning for us. A n-new door to step through..." Her voice broke and a tear rolled down her cheek.

Clara and Dad appeared next to us. Dad looked at me and gave me his warmest smile while he comforted Mom. Mom was right. Sometimes things couldn't stay the way we wanted them to stay, and when things change, people must adapt. I looked at Clara. Her face was discolored.

"Let's go..." she said.

And we walked up to our new house.

I took a deep breath as Dad picked up the fake mushroom key hider and took out the silver, rusted key. He unlocked the door, and we crossed the threshold into our new life. I was instantly shocked. The house was made of a light brown wood, and it was kind of dirty. Although it did have a few white cabinets lining the living room, and the kitchen facing north, which Mom found very auspicious, it didn't quite seem like home. I finally saw the elegant birch wood stairs and some doors upstairs. *This is all so cool!* I thought. *But can I ever live here?*

The materials of the house weren't made from leaves or any other natural items, which I found interesting. I used to sleep in a cozy cat bed and a hammock back in our cottage in Animalia, where I also used to hide away in cat towers all day with Clara. *Speaking of Clara...*I glanced at my elder sister. She seemed to be taking a liking to the house.

"This place is nice! Not bad at all," she said.

I grinned. Mom and Dad watched us, beaming.

"Well, girls, this is a new beginning! Tomorrow, we can make this house feel like home!" Dad winked. "We'll also get a chance to check out your new school!"

My head drooped. *I can't just go to a human school...they're so different from me. And what about Hazel? I have no idea if she survived the volcano or not...She always spoke so strongly about how her family disapproved of Humania...If I met her again sometime, would she still like me?*

***

That night, as I settled down on the couch, trying to sleep, I couldn't think about anything or anyone except for Hazel and

Mount Anaconda and Animalia. I tried to think good thoughts, like making new friends or exploring the forests around Small Town. The thought of having a Humanian bed tomorrow calmed the butterflies in my stomach a little.

    However, I still hardly got any sleep that first night.

CHAPTER 2

Small patches of sunlight hit my face, and I sat up on the couch. I threw my blanket to the floor and hopped out of bed. My eyes had black bags under them, and I couldn't do anything but yawn.

When I entered the kitchen, I could hear the muffled voices of Mom and Dad talking about ways to earn money here from their bedroom. I realized that I had forgotten we had just arrived and needed to find a living in our new town.

I walked up the fridge, my feet dragging behind me like a zombie. I guessed I looked like a skinny stray cat, starving for food. I rubbed my eyes and reached for the cereal instinctively on the right shelf, but my hands grasped thin air. *Oh right...We don't have any more Cinnamon Koala Crisps here...*

Before the eruption, Mom always bought a fresh pack every month, as they were my favorite kind of cereal. Clara's too. At the shelter, a rich Animalian who had been away from home during the eruption generously donated some. But

The Cat of Small Town

Cinnamon Koala Crisps were a product of Animalia, so I doubted they sold them here in Small Town.

I sighed and grabbed a milk carton that we had unloaded from our trunk yesterday. I sniffed it, then immediately recoiled at the dirty gym sock aroma.

"Ew!" I covered my nostrils.

I suddenly looked back at the living room. My parent's voices had become more worried sounding. I stayed out of sight and sat next to the slightly open door, trying to eavesdrop on their conversation.

"How are we going to find a place to work that will earn us a steady income? Marty, I'm seriously feeling hopeless right now..." Mom's voice drifted into my ears.

I started to shake, but I kept listening.

"I'll try to use my talents? I've always had a passion for music...Will that work, Allison?" Dad asked in a low voice.

"*You're asking me?*" Mom's voice was quite shrill. "You were in charge of everything that was financial for when we moved here!"

I could tell they were both trying to hide their worry, unsuccessfully, if you asked me.

What if Mom or Dad can't find a job…What could I do then? If they can't find anywhere to work, how will we keep paying to live here? My thoughts swirled in my head and mixed up like soup. I was dizzy from all the cold thoughts spreading throughout my mind all at once.

I'll be fine. Everything will be alright, I assured myself. I shooed all of the bad thoughts out of my brain and took a deep, deep breath.

Suddenly, I felt someone grab my shoulders and squeeze.

"Ah-" I yelled, but Clara shushed me and got on her knees beside the door as well.

"Be quiet! You don't want them to catch us, do you?" Clara said bossily.

"Well, don't sneak up on people! That just makes them make noise, don't you know?" I replied harshly.

"Er…" Clara began. "Just let me listen, would you?"

We put our ears to the door and listened again.

I could hear Mom sobbing.

"It-It broke me when Mama died...The kids-they loved their Granny so much...I wish all of this never happened..." Mom said through sharp breaths.

My eyes widened, and I glanced at Clara. She was trying hard to fight her tears as well. I locked eyes with my sister, who also had a damp face. I tried to stand and walk into the kitchen, but I couldn't get up. It was as if someone had glued me to the floor. I looked at Clara for help, but before we could do anything, the door started to open. I gasped.

Suddenly, Mom's familiar face came into view above us. She looked down for a split second and her eyes widened. Then, she accidentally tripped over one of Clara's wings and went flying.

"AH!" she screamed.

Dad tried to grab for her, but it was too late, and moments later, Mom was sprawled face-first on the floor.

"Mom!" I cried.

Thankfully, Mom was alright. She got steadily to her feet, but her gaze turned firm.

"Mom...?" Clara asked.

"What were you two doing outside of our door?" she inquired, a bit harshly.

"...Uh...err...we..."

I couldn't utter any words. They couldn't come out, and it felt as if someone had stuffed a huge rock into my mouth.

"Alright, it's okay. Today, we are going to get a few things unpacked. Let's all be happy today, and let's not try to shout or yell at each other, alright?" said Dad.

I secretly thanked him, and he winked playfully at me.

Mom and Dad walked outside like they planned, leaving Clara and me at the doorstep. A few minutes later, a large *whirr* sound pulled into our little house's driveway. A man with hairy arms and a hard hat greeted my parents and got down from the moving van. I watched them talk for a bit, then the man's assistants began to unload the furniture from the van's trunk. We ran over to help, but each box was as heavy as a rock. I saw Clara get the box that held all her books and toys that she used to read and play with. Some of them were falling apart, and some were halfway burned to crisps, but Clara insisted on keeping them.

    I chose a package that had a stool, glass cups, and pans that were all very delicate. I thought my arms would fall off after only a few steps. But I managed to walk slowly back into the house, shifting the weight of the box to each arm. I crossed the front yard, dodging the fountain, but I couldn't see where I was going since the stacked boxes blocked my line of sight. Suddenly, there was a huge CRASH! I couldn't feel the enormous boxes in my grasp anymore. It happened too fast for me to see the boxes flying up.

    Pots and pans crashed together as they flew up into the sky. The glass cups smashed together in midair and shattered into pieces. They seemed to be in slow motion as they began to fall. Then, they sped up again. One large pot came down on my head, and I was sure I could still hear it vibrating inside my poor skull. I caught a glimpse of Clara's books and toys soaring in the air as well, and we fell to the ground.

Moments later, we were sprawled on the path that led up to the front door, and Mom ran up to us.

"ARE YOU GIRLS OKAY?" she asked frantically.

She stuck a hand out to help us up. "You girls are masters of disasters. I'm just so very glad you're okay..."

"Heh," I said, giving Clara a hard glare, hoping Mom wouldn't notice while I rubbed my ears, hoping the pain would dissipate.

The hairy man and Dad walked up to us, frowning. The man said something to Dad and then walked back to his truck, yelling orders at his colleagues. Soon, the moving van left us in the dust with multiple boxes and appliances scattered around our front yard.

Mom glanced at us wearily, and Dad sighed. "Alright, let's carry these boxes to the rooms they belong to. No delay!"

***

We spent the next few hours getting the boxes inside the house and putting them in the rooms they had belonged in until we couldn't stand up on our feet anymore. I fell from the pain in my knees from carrying tons of boxes up and down the stairs. Thankfully, Mom put some cooling cream on my joints and the pain subsided.

At four o' clock, we collapsed on the couch and relaxed, but Mom suddenly looked at the clock on the wall. "Clara, Penelope-put on your shoes! We need to hurry! Your school's open house today!"

She waved the crumpled school open house flier in her hands as her fluffy tail waved frantically.

We jumped off the couch and hurried to put on our shoes. I was super nervous, and I didn't want to go at all. However, the other part of me was sort of excited.

I ran to the car, my black slippers halfway on, and we sped away into the evening. During the car ride, I was ecstatic to meet my teachers and see my school, but butterflies were also fluttering around in my stomach.

We arrived a few minutes later, and I gasped as I took in the huge two-story school. It was made of beautiful white bricks and shimmering blue windows. The name of the school, *SEPTEMBER DAWN ACADEMY*, was engraved at the top in huge black letters. There was a small garden that had a swing and was also full of posies, daffodils, sunflowers, and wild roses at the back of the school next to the bus loop. Brown benches were scattered around, and a small basketball court had been placed on the left side of the huge building.

    I scanned the entrance of the school. A lot of families were walking towards the huge door, and I heard children yelling and laughing cheerfully as they entered their new school. I looked up at my mother with glowing, hopeful eyes as I squeezed her hand. She smiled at me, and I grinned. Clara was looking around in amazement of how beautiful the academy was. It felt as if I was back at my old school at Animalia, even though the teachers used to slap a ruler to our knuckles if we were naughty, and some of them barely cared about doing their jobs. They often never wanted to know about our home lives, and I hoped the teachers here in Humania would be different.

A chubby blonde boy caught my attention. His parents, even more chubby, walked beside him as he licked a huge popsicle from one of the ice cream stands at the entrance. He glanced in my direction, and he glowered at me. I immediately became interested in my half-worn slippers. *I hope that boy isn't in my class...*

My eyes lingered on another boy, one with messy brown hair, green eyes, and thick framed glasses and he seemed to be holding a book in one of his hands. He instantly caught my attention, and I couldn't tear my eyes away from him. The boy was asking the teachers all sorts of questions about September Dawn.

Suddenly, I heard a teacher snap at him, "Stop asking logical questions that can answer themselves, would *you*?"

The boy looked slightly embarrassed, and he shut his mouth. I felt a wave of pity wash over me as I forced myself to look away from the scene as we entered the school.

The inside of the school is huge! I realized.

All around us were tons of doors, all marked with a plate that stated the class and grade number.

Mom looked at me. "Penelope, your dad, Clara, and I will go look upstairs and down the hallway that leads to eighth grade, where Clara will be. Please stay at the library over there."

She pointed at one of the doors on the right side of the hall. I nodded and walked inside without another word. The library doors seemed small, so I had expected the library itself to be just as cramped. But when I entered, my ears immediately flicked this way and that. The library was *enormous. It must take up at least a third of the school...* I thought.

I traversed slowly through each shelf, passing through the fantasy section and the biographies and the graphic novels. I was mesmerized.

Suddenly, I entered the nonfiction shelves. My eyes lingered on a book about Animalians. It was titled, *The World of Half-Animals: Animalians and their Customs by Shannon B.* I reached out for it and slid it off the shelf. The cover showed a picture of a human and a bear Animalian standing back-to-back.

I didn't think I stared at the cover for very long, but a snarl behind me made me whip around in surprise. "Who-w-what?"

The chubby boy I had seen earlier slapped the book out of my hand, and it clattered onto the patterned carpet that was placed on the floor.

"What do you think you're doing, Fat *Freak*?"

"I-"

He grabbed the book and shoved it in my face. "*Your* type *doesn't* belong here."

I looked down at my feet. "I know. But I can't go home." An air of confidence suddenly drifted into me. "It's not every day a volcano erupts and destroys everything you love, you know, pudgy glutton."

Oops, I thought. When did I think of that insult? Nevermind, just get ready to get punched, Penelope.

However, instead of resorting to violence, the boy looked a bit shocked, and I gently pulled the book out of his hand. I slipped it back onto its shelf and walked away. *Why can't people understand, though...?*

I walked outside the school building, even though Mom instructed me to wait in the library. I just couldn't stand being inside that environment for too long. I needed some fresh air.

I walked over to the garden near the bus loop that had so many different types of flowers in it. Suddenly, I saw something move next to a cherry blossom tree.

A quiet and calm voice suddenly broke the silence and said, "Hello there, are you planning to go to this school? Anyways, this cherry blossom looks just like the one back at my little cottage."

I turned around quickly to see who was speaking, but a thick layer of mist had spread around me.

I know there was someone there... I stared at the mist for a few moments before it dissolved into the light. *Or maybe my brain was playing tricks on me...*

I sped back toward the entrance, knowing that my parents and sister would be looking for me in the library soon. I ignored the strange looks I received from the human families and ran down the hall. I stumbled into the library and caught my breath. Thankfully, the boy was gone, and my family just happened to peek in a moment later.

"We're back!" Mom exclaimed. "How did you like the library? It sure is huge."

I took a deep breath and said, "It-It was nice."

Dad seemed to notice something was wrong in my tone, though. "Penelope did someone give you any trouble?" he asked calmly, as if he had experienced getting bullied for his appearance too.

Then again, I thought. *Dad went to college here, so that could be true.*

"No, I just want to go home right now, that's why," I said, trying to not look suspicious.

"Okay then, let's go home!" said Dad cheerfully. "Unfortunately, we asked if the fifth grade classes had been announced yet, but they were delayed. We'll find out soon enough."

Clara, Mom, and I nodded. We set out for the car, and I felt glad we were finally going back home after a chaotic open house.

***

I ran over to the couch in our small living room as soon as we arrived home.

Clara took a seat next to me. "So did you like September Dawn Academy?" she asked gently.

"It was nice..." I said, staring at my feet. "Did you like it?" I asked a few moments later.

She looked at me happily. "The eighth grade hallway was really cool!" She smiled.

"Oh...nice..."

At least Clara had a good evening...I hope I won't see that bully again.

CHAPTER 3

The first day of school arrived faster than I thought it would. I had gotten school supplies that I needed for 5th grade from a store nearby our house. I changed out of my white t-shirt and into my black-and-white school uniform that I had gotten recently. As soon as I pulled it over my head, I immediately wanted to unsheath my nails and tear it to shreds.

It-It's SO itchy... I complained inside.

I looked around my room. There was only a bed and a few clothes laying on it. The small window in my room showered enough sunlight to get me ready for the big day. I opened my door and walked down the stairs. Just when I stepped into the kitchen the smell of fresh baked pancakes practically made me float over to the table.

"Good morning, Sunshine," said Dad, glancing up from his computer as I entered the kitchen.

"Hey, Dad," I said, sliding into a stool at the table beside Clara.

Clara shoved a pancake into her mouth and turned to Mom, who was still flipping pancakes at the stove.

"*Hey* Mom," she said, talking with food still in her mouth. "It's our ferst day at school, right?"

Mom chuckled. "Yes. Are you girls excited?"

I hesitated, but said, "Yeah. Yeah, I'm excited."

I sure hoped I was.

After breakfast, I walked up to my dad's car slower than a snail. Mom would be dropping Clara to school today, so I had to go with Dad.

"Alright, let's go!" exclaimed Dad when I threw the car door open and sat down on the soft, comfy seats.

The engine started and we drove to September Dawn.

***

I shouldered my backpack as I walked through the doors to the school, which was a pure, ashy black color. I was quite unhappy about this forced choice since I wanted to take my pastel purple backpack that I had saved from Animalia instead. I was still grateful that I had a backpack because I didn't think I would manage to carry all my supplies to school without one. Would I get to carry all of them in my hands? Thinking about all this made chills run down my spine. I shook my head. *I must focus on surviving my first day at a human school*, I reminded myself as I took a deep breath and passed by the welcome banners.

    I traversed down the halls, trying to ignore the sideways looks the other students were giving me. Some parts of Humania barely had heard about Animalia and Animalians, so I tried to think of the phrase, "People who are rude usually don't like anything different from themselves."

    I caught a group of older girls whispering and giggling at my ears and tail, and I rushed past them stormily. *Why does it have to be so hard? I've just entered the school, and thanks be, who knows how I'm going to get past a whole entire school year?*

    I found my classroom, Room 24, which had been emailed to my parents yesterday, and I didn't know what to expect because I hadn't been introduced to my teacher during the open house. I stepped through the door, and my ears immediately recoiled at the blur of noise and chaos in the classroom. Clearly, my new teacher didn't know how to keep order.

To my dismay, the chubby boy, who I later found out to be named Brandon, from the open house was tackling one of my classmates with poorly dyed rainbow hair. Some other boys were shooting spitballs and paper airplanes across the room, and a group of pretty girls practically drowning in makeup were fanning their faces at the sight of the guys, and I grimaced.

Then, the shine of glasses caught my eye. I turned, and immediately recognized the brown-haired boy with the glasses, sitting in a corner, reading a thick novel. He caught my gaze and suddenly looked up at me. I looked away, and suddenly everyone seemed to realize the fact that I was *there*.

The group of girls gave me a cat eye, looking me over from tail to ears. I felt self-conscious, and my face burned. I finally caught a glimpse of my teacher behind all the commotion. She was a plain faced, but rosy-cheeked woman with messy brown hair and a pencil holding her bun together. She was hastily flipping through her teacher's notes pinned smartly on a clipboard, and she didn't take notice of me at first. However, I was clueless as to where to hang my backpack, so I cautiously approached her.

"Hello," I began.

She looked up, and her strikingly hopeful, yellow eyes made a jolt run through my body. She didn't say anything for a moment or two, and she studied my face, trying to see if she remembered me or not from a past life.

"Ah," she finally spoke. "Petunia, right? How lovely to meet you. I've heard a lot about you, little miss."

"It's 'Penelope'," I corrected. "Nice to meet you."

My teacher smiled. "Sorry, sorry, it's just that I'm usually so over the place on the first day of school. Yes, dear, wonderful to finally meet you. I'm Mrs. Gwendolen Firewood. Hang your backpack over there, dearie, and your name should be at your seat. I'll be here if you need me."

I nodded, and when I turned my back to her to hang up my bookbag at the hangers in the back of the room, I smiled secretly. *Mrs. Firewood is an oddity, but she sure seems eccentric.* I looked for my name, and some of my classmates glared at me as my eyes darted across the tables. Suddenly, I found mine, across from the brown-haired boy. I cautiously sat down, but I had no reason to be afraid.

The boy seemed like a kindred spirit, and as soon as I settled in my seat, he turned to me. "You must be an Animalian," he stated, quite bluntly.

I was shocked at his sudden remark, but I replied as politely as I could, "Yeah...I am. How did you know the name of the place I'm from?" I couldn't stop myself from raising my eyebrows.

"I've read a few books about Animalians and the island. For example, the humans that wound up on the island so long ago were blessed by the nature spirits and everything in it, with animal parts," he said, grinning like a smart aleck, which he apparently was.

"Oh, wow, did you read every single page of every single book in the library?" I joked.

I couldn't help but start grinning too. Talking to him wasn't hard at all, I didn't have to try my best to start a conversation. Words just came out of my mouth like water when I spoke to him. Suddenly I realized that I hadn't introduced myself to the guy.

"I'm Penelope," I smiled. "I'm sorry that I forgot to introduce myself,"

"I'm Jeremy," he said, and I immediately knew I wouldn't have quite as bad a time at September Dawn as I expected.

CHAPTER 4

The day whizzed past, from beginning the day with a boring lesson on decimals and fractions and a quite energizing but embarrassing reading group session. The other kids in my group included Jeremy, a girl named Felicia Reynolds, and a boy named Ivan Walkerman. Felicia kept whispering to Ivan about my classic Animalian accent, and my face was as red as a tomato when I finished reading my paragraph. Thankfully, Mrs. Firewood supported me all the way.

Eons later, Mrs. Firewood announced that we would have Physical Education as our resource today, and I was excited to have a break from the hard plastic chairs in the classroom. However, I had no idea how things would take a turn from there.

***

When it was finally time to go to the gym for P.E. I realized beads of sweat dotted my forehead. I was excited at first to get a break from sitting still, but P.E. teachers were always unpredictable and would yell at you for the smallest things. I was afraid a million things would go wrong. We had been forced to change into special P.E. jerseys and black shorts, which were just as uncomfortable as the uniforms.

Mrs. Firewood showed us our line order, and thanks to my luck, Jeremy was in front of me, but just when my mood lightened, I realized that Brandon was behind me in line. Mrs. Firwood dropped us off at the huge gym, and I was afraid to see her go. She was the only one who would take my side, apart from Jeremy.

"Have fun!" said Mrs. Firewood as she left, and all of us quickly walked into the gym.

Everyone in the line whispered and some were talking loudly. Some didn't even notice Mrs. Firewood leaving, and I felt a hot lump of anger expanding in my throat for a strange reason. Then, a strangely high voice from a side door in the gym commanded us to sit down on the cold, shockingly spotless gym floor. I sat down, and I felt a hand move behind me.

I flinched when Brandon yanked on my tail. My eyes started to water, and I almost stumbled and hit my head on the floor.

Suddenly, combat boots stomped into the room. Our P.E. teacher was at least 10 feet tall, and she had huge muscles and a red t-shirt that read, "Coffee Is NOT My Bestie". I slowly looked up from her XXL shorts and stared at her face for a few seconds. She had a huge bald spot in the middle of her head, and she seemed to have pale blonde hair that almost looked green. Her locks of hair were cut unevenly, and her eyes were set far apart and were as tiny as beetle shells. Her nose was as sharp as a witch's, but as I stared at the little hairs under it, I almost began to giggle.

"ATTENTION!" yelled the strange P.E. instructor. "I am Mrs. Fatbeard."

Felicia, a few feet away from me, let out a hysterical laugh. Her friend elbowed her vigorously, alarm crowding their faces.

Mrs. Fatbeard glared at Felicia. "Get up, young lady."

Felicia's face reddened with embarrassment. She steadily got to her feet and walked towards Mrs. Fatbeard.

"You will demonstrate the next exercise. Run 20 laps around the gym so your classmates can get an idea for the race we're about to do," she said, in her high-strung voice of hers.

I gasped. *20 laps?* I watched Felicia run around the gym for six minutes, but soon she seemed to be out of breath from running for some time. She panted when she finally completed all the laps. "So, as you can see everyone you will be doing the exact same thing that...err...Mariam Dunbery Douglas III-" she guessed.

"Felicia," she corrected.

"Whatever. So, you will be doing what she did, understand, zucchinis?"

Everyone nodded, and I tried to hold myself together after she called us "zucchinis".

I started getting up to do the 20 laps with everyone else, but a hand pulled me back and said, "Are you going to try to run, Cat Freak? Creatures like you shouldn't be allowed to even walk on this land."

I realized it was Brandon.

Everyone in the gym except Mrs. Fatbeard, who was too busy eating her food, looked at us. Brandon smirked at me, and I felt sick to my stomach...I tried to hold my tears and my anger back. I tried to avert my gaze from him. But I couldn't, as hard as I tried. *I am fast...right? I am half cat. I-I should be...I always beat Hazel back in...Animalia...*

My thoughts made me feel the pain worse than his words. I was terrible at hiding my emotions, and I felt helpless. I decided to let every rude thing he said wash over me.

Suddenly, the door of the gym slammed open and a girl with misty blue eyes and light brown hair that shined like the sun appeared in the doorway. A teacher I assumed was a counselor walked in next to her. The counselor whispered something to the girl and spoke to Mrs. Fatbeard and left.

I caught some of their conversation, and I pretty much forgot Brandon was there.

"We found her...It's illegal for children her age not to go to school..."

"So...are you sad? You're going to cry?" said Brandon, startling me out of my concentration.

Before I could say anything or burst into tears, the girl strutted up to Brandon. Everyone turned to her direction. She seemed to have clearly picked up on the situation, and she sure didn't seem happy about it. I was always scared of angry people, but for some reason, I felt something deep inside me assure me that she wouldn't hurt me.

Her face was so pale, she looked like a living ghost. Her black leather shoes were peeling on the soles and ripped. Her socks didn't look very new either. Her uniform top was tucked inside her skirt, which was probably against the dress code, and some parts of it hung loosely on the sides.

The front parts of her hair were pulled back into a braid at the back of her head, and a cherry blossom adorned her head. She looked a bit taller than me, and much more frightening.

"Hey, you!" She got right in Brandon's face, and her eyes flared. "You're jealous! Girls can run fast. Faster than you'll ever be! You'll only wish to run as fast as us! And don't underestimate someone who's a bit different than you, understand?"

Brandon's face was as red as a sun-dried tomato. He seemed embarrassed a girl showed him up in front of everyone.

"Whatever!" he yelled.

He stomped away to do his laps. Everyone stopped staring and resumed running, but still shot the girl inquisitive looks now and then.

I was shocked. This-this girl had helped me. I glanced at her, and she looked me in the eye. Her blue irises twinkled, but looked as if she had something sad buried deep within. She gave me a warm smile just like Clara used to before the eruption. Something about her tone and voice reminded me of something that had happened earlier, but I couldn't get a grip on what it was.

I finally managed to open my mouth. "Excuse me? Thank you for helping me."

"Of course! I'm Lilith, what's your name?" the girl replied kindly.

"That's a lovely name! I'm Penelope Wilder? From Animalia..." I said slowly.

"Thank you and your name shimmers like the stars! I can tell. I've read about Animalia in my mom's library in our house," Lilith said.

She stared at her feet, and I had a tiny inkling that she didn't like to talk about her mother. *She is really kind...But she does seem lonely...*

"Do you want to be my friend?" Lilith asked suddenly, breaking the silence. I was surprised by the hint in her voice that she was prepared if I said "no".

"Yes! I would love to be your friend!" I grinned.

Lilith suddenly looked up with those misty, hopeful eyes of hers. She smiled.

Suddenly, I realized that Jeremy was behind me. I turned around. "Lilith, meet my friend Jeremy. Jeremy, this is Lilith!"

"Hi!" Lilith stuck out her hand, and Jeremy shook it respectfully.

"Hello," he replied genially.

I was about to ask Lilith something, but Mrs. Fatbeard gave us a death stare and accidently spit out some of her coffee. "STOP STANDING AROUND AND TALKING AND RUN!"

I shrugged and tried to stop myself from laughing. Lilith and Jeremy were looking as if they were trying to stop themselves too. I knew from then on that I would have wonderful adventures with these kindred spirits. I smiled and ran to complete the laps with Lilith and Jeremy.

***

Some people think lunchtime as a social time for people to talk and eat with their friends. I considered lunchtime as a gift from God that gives me a much needed break and enjoy the day with our friends and classmates. And earlier, I didn't think that I'd *ever* have a friend at September Dawn, but I was proud of myself-and grateful-for earning Jeremy and Lilith's companionship so early in the school year.

Mrs. Firewood instructed the class to enter the huge cafeteria, and I was immediately blinded by the neon pink walls and some white bricks. I covered my eyes, muttering under my breath, "This school sure doesn't have any theme colors…Pristine white on the outside, pink inside?"

Lilith giggled. "That's true."

My teacher put a gentle hand on my shoulder and guided me through the lunch line. I grabbed Menu Option 2, tacos, and looked down as the fat old lunch lady scowled at me. She placed the taco on my tray scornfully, and I quickly grabbed some sugary pineapples and a cookie and quickly exited the line. There were too many children in the cafeteria, all immediately falling silent as I passed them with my tray. Some whispered, pointing at my appearance and laughing. Some seemed confused and kept their mouths shut.

I slid into a seat beside Lilith and across from Jeremy, and I was immediately relieved from the experience. I set down my tray and picked up on the conversation Jeremy was having with Lilith.

"Did you know that elephants aren't really afraid of rats? They actually..." Jeremy blabbed on and on.

Lilith nodded, although I wasn't quite sure if she understood anything Jeremy was saying.

I took a big bite out of my taco. "Do you guys like the first day of school so far?" I asked, smiling.

"Yeah, it sure is good...I'm glad we all became friends. I didn't think I would make any, to be honest," said Lilith, looking down at her healthy-looking salad and the mochi on the side. I regretted taking the taco for lunch since my mouth began to water at the mochi.

"I'm liking the first day of school. This is my fifth year here at September Dawn, actually. My parents sent me here ever since kindergarten. Oh, and did you guys know that some schools are more than 20 years old? This one is more than a century old I think...The history on how it came about is quite interesting, too," said Jeremy, matter-of-factly.

A century old!

"Wow, that's a long time to be here...I-I just arrived here in

Humania...Anyways, a century?" I asked in disbelief.

Suddenly Felicia slid into a seat next to me, "Oh wow, it's that old? I don't think that's true, Jeremy. You're *such* a big liar, you know that?" she smirked and placed a cold hand on my shoulder. I wanted to pry it off, but I became silent and looked down at my taco.

Jeremy suddenly became interested in his book, and his face burned, probably of shame or embarrassment. I glanced at Lilith, who was taking a bite of her mochi. Her face seemed quite serene, but her misty eyes turned stormy.

"I think *you* are the liar," said Lilith.

I gasped and whipped around to see how Felicia would respond. Felicia stood up and glowered at Lilith.

Then, she threw her head back and gave a startling laugh. "Hah! Me, a liar, lit-little poor girl? Look at your clothes, your shoes! Were they chewed up by a shark then thrown up before you wore them? What about your parents? They don't seem to be around, do they? Oh, did something *bad* happen to them? They must have been so ashamed to have given birth to you, right?"

I gasped. The insults hadn't been meant for me, but I felt like crying nonetheless. I looked to Lilith hopefully. *Please don't give her the reaction she wants from you.* I tried to send a telepathic message to her brain.

Suddenly, Lilith turned to me and smiled. She nodded, and her eyes turned cold.

"No," she said, surprisingly softly to Felicia.

Something seemed to come over the bully. She made a "humph" sound and trotted off to sit next to her friends Verda and Simona, but Mrs. Fatbeard, passing by, grabbed her by her ear and started a conversation over dumbbells in the cafeteria hallway. I stared after Felicia in wonder for a bit, but then slowly turned to Lilith.

"H-How did you do that? St-Standing up for yourself, I mean. Not even *yourself*! For us!" I asked in disbelief.

Lilith turned to me and smiled, and I was surprised. I beamed back. I was glad to have a friend like her and Jeremy.

***

"How was your first day of school, honey?" asked Mom as I threw the door open, dropped my backpack across the wood floor, and jumped on the couch.

"It was good," I replied plainly.

Mom walked up to me and handed me a fresh-baked muffin. "No, no! I want the details, Penny."

Penny. Hazel's face suddenly flooded my brain, and I stared, wide-eyed into space for a few moments, remembering each time she referred to me as "Penny", and what was going on during that moment. Tears suddenly trickled down my cheeks, but I didn't even wail. I buried my face on my legs on the couch and wiped my eyes in silence.

Mom noticed. She sat down next to me on the couch, and she placed a gentle hand on my shoulder. Mom didn't say anything, but I was so close to her that we could exchange thoughts without words.

"I miss Hazel too," said Mom, softly. "I didn't mean to remind you of her, Penelope. I'm sorry...There's still hope she made it out...Even though she wasn't at the shelter we had to stay at, that doesn't mean she's gone for good..."

I turned to look at Mom. Ever so slowly, tears dripped down her wet face as well. I flung my arms around her, and we both cried until we didn't have any energy left to keep doing so.

Clara found us, sitting there on the couch with our arms around each other when she came back from school at four.

"Hey!" She stopped short when she noticed our sad faces. "Why are you two moping around?"

I snapped my head up. "I miss Animalia. I miss everything," I explained hopelessly.

"Well don't pout about it. We're here now, and the past is in the past," preached Clara.

Mom smiled at my sister and pointed to me. "Penelope tells me she's made some friends already."

I explained everything that had happened, leaving out the parts with Brandon and Felicia. I didn't want to make them worry about me and possibly choose to send me to another school, as I had just made some amazing friends.

    Clara and Mom laughed their heads off as I told them about Mrs. Fatbeard, and Mom listened intently when I told her about Lilith and Jeremy. Mom smiled knowingly when I told her about how Mrs. Firewood would always have my back, and she patted me gently on the head when I had finished.

    "What a day, Penelope!" she exclaimed. "How exciting...I wish schools were like that when I was young, and in your old school, too."

    Clara scoffed, but I decided to make her uncomfortable by asking, "Meet anyone *special*?"

    Clara blushed hot pink and fake-coughed. "*What?* You're too young and *unsmart* to understand that stuff."

    Mom chuckled. "Clara, sweetie, help me prepare supper, would you?"

    Clara got up from the couch to assist Mom in the kitchen, and I was left reflecting on the day for a few minutes.

CHAPTER 5

The next day of school, I made sure to carry around an electronic watch to school just in case I had to smash the SOS button, for there were *so* many things that could go wrong on the second day of school.

I walked into the classroom, hoping I looked as fresh as a daisy, but I looked like a kid who woke up late to school and had to get ready for school in three milliseconds.

"Morning," I said, drowsily, to Jeremy, who was always the first one in the classroom.

"Morning!" he replied, then brought a finger to his lips and kept reading his 7,000 page book on the anatomy of amphibians.

I hung up my backpack and took a seat at my desk, shifting through the Morning Work papers in front of me. I chose a page I'd like to do, but before I could even grab a pencil from my supplies box, the bell rang, and the school announcements started on the electronic board.

"Everyone, up!" Mrs. Firewood instructed. "Time for the anthem."

Humania's pledge suddenly erupted from the screen, but it sounded very different from the Animalian one, which was in our native tongue. I tried to copy what my other classmates were doing: getting down on one knee and saying the pledge under their breath.

However, when I tried to get down on one knee, I tripped over my tail and my head, and my desk collided with an unpleasant *BANG!*

Everyone turned to look at me, and Lilith rushed forward to help me to my feet. By now, I had missed the pledge and the anthem began to play.

> "Ring, ring, the bells must ring,
> the streams must run, oh so far,
> let the buffalo run, down by the shore,
> houses built here an' there,
> working hard by the stare,
> in this fair ol' land of ours."

The anthem stopped, and everyone got back to their feet. I felt embarrassed that I could not sing along with them. The song was quite nice, and I set a goal for myself: I would learn the anthem, even if it took me all school year.

A few boring lessons and mean remarks from Felicia later, Mrs. Firewood announced we would be starting a big project today. She explained that we would get in groups of three, and mail letters to random addresses in Animalia, to explain how we supported the effort and resilience of the Animalians as they pushed through the disaster that recently occurred. I looked down at my feet, hoping that everyone wasn't looking at me.

"So!" yelled Mrs. Firewood, startling the class. "I will tell you who your partners for the groups tomorrow will be after the announcements."

My eyes were shining, and I hoped that I would get to be in a group with Lilith and Jeremy.

Mrs. Firewood told us to get our binders and our math notebooks. "Okay, so today we are going to be introduced to algebra!" said Mrs. Firewood, as she took a few papers out of one of the shelves next to her desk space and passed out the sheets across the classroom.

Everyone groaned, but I was quite excited. Back in Animalia, I had been an ace at solving algebraic problems. We all took our seats and I stared at the paper that Mrs. Firewood had given and glanced around the classroom. Some kids were scratching their heads and complaining about how hard the problems looked. The problems didn't seem too hard to me.

In Animalia, they taught some quick methods for solving different equations, and I got the answer for each of the questions in a few seconds. I barely had to use the scratch paper Mrs. Firewood passed around.

I realized that I was the first one to finish, so I got up to grab a book to read while I waited for everyone else to finish. When I returned to my seat, I saw Brandon snatch my sheet from my desk and copy from it. Before I could affront him, he scampered away. I quietly tore the paper into shreds and recycled it. Everyone was so obsessed with their work that they didn't notice.

My face burning with shame and anger, I kindly asked Mrs. Firewood for another sheet, but the disappointed and confused look she gave me made my heart melt.

***

Later, Mrs. Firewood announced that today's resource class would be library time, and I was excited to put my hands on some cool books written by Humanian authors, although I could tell I wasn't as excited as Jeremy. Mrs. Firewood told us to line up at the door, and out of our classroom we went, passing the third and fourth grade hallways. Soon, we walked up to the same small doors I had entered during the open house.

We knocked, and a pretty woman with chocolaty brown eyes and a pink smile greeted us. She had short black hair that was tied into small little braids on either side of her shoulders, and she had some pretty cat-eye glasses stuck onto her nose.

"Class, for those who are new here, this is Mrs. Bridgeton. She's the school librarian, and make sure to treat her with respect. Capisce?"

"Capisce." My face turned red when I realized I was the only one who said this.

Then, Mrs. Firewood strutted back down the hall and left us with Mrs. Bridgeton. The kindly librarian led us inside and instructed us to sit down at one of the round tables in a small room at the heart of all the bookshelves.

I sat down with Jeremy and Lilith, and I immediately scanned the curved bookshelves around me for any of my all-time favorites. However, all the books in sight seemed almost alien to me, and I turned away.

Mrs. Bridgeton explained to us the basic rules of being in the school library: be respectful, listen, treat the books kindly, and don't ever run. Then, she clapped her hands. Everyone stood up and Mrs. Bridgeton instructed us to look around.

"Two books at a time," she said.

Jeremy made a dash for the books that were labeled "5th Grade Only", which he explained hurriedly that he'd been waiting for forever to read. Lilith seemed as confused as I was, since she was also new to the school. Together, we walked through the bookshelves, occasionally pulling a few from each shelf to read their summaries.

    I suddenly remembered the two Animalian books I had seen at the open house. I had only been able to look at one, but I wanted to check out both of them to see what humans thought of Animalians. I walked into the non-fiction section and found the place where the books were. However, the one I hadn't looked at had disappeared from the shelf. *Maybe someone checked it out...*I grabbed *The World of Half-Animals: Animalians and their Customs.*

    Suddenly, Brandon came into view behind a bookshelf nearby. He was whispering and pointing meanly at the contents of the book in his hands to Felicia. I read the spine from afar with my excellent cat vision: *Terrifying Beings: Animalians and their Monstrous Traits and Disabilities.*

    I shivered. I was glad I had grabbed a seemingly kinder book about Animalians. I wandered off to see the graphic novel section when a large

The Cat of Small Town

commotion attracted my attention. *I guess I'll just take this book today,* I decided, shifting the weight of *The World of Half Animals: Animalians and their Customs* in my hands.

I peeked over Lilith's tall shoulder. Everyone was making impressions of Animalians as Brandon read out the contents of the pages of his book. I turned on my heel and stomped over to Mrs. Heartman, the assistant librarian, who checked out my book.

"Angry?" Mrs. Heartman inquired.

"Nope," I said, a bit downheartedly.

"Alright..."

***

On the bus home, I tried to avoid sitting in the back of the bus because Brandon was still reading that terrible book and making fun of Animalians with his dumb friends. I remembered the advice Jeremy had told me, "When in doubt, crack open a book".

I opened the first page of *The World of Half-Animals: Animalians and their Customs* and read:

The Cat of Small Town

"Introduction

Animalians, seeing from their names, are half human, half animal. All of them share common ancestors. At least four centuries ago, a group of 60 or so humans decided to be passengers with Captain Beasely on his ship, September Dawn. Only after a few days of voyage, a huge storm threw the ship south, and they landed on an abandoned island that would soon be called Animalia. The humans had to learn the ways of nature and to survive, and the goddess of nature, Calla, gifted them with the animal traits they have today."

At the bottom of the first page, there was an old, faded portrait of Captain Beasely and his ship which my school had been named after. The bus stopped and I realized it was time for me to get off. I quickly walked outside, trying to avoid the ugly and disrespectful faces that Brandon and his friends were making at me at the bus stop. As I speed-walked back home, I opened the next page in the book.

"Animalians Today and in Recent Times

Animalians usually live in houses that suit their animal characteristics best, for example, bird Animalians would live in huge nests and would decorate them expertly with many leaves, flowers, and branches with their crafting skills. Some huge families that have many kinds of different Animalians, since there are no hybrid Animalians. These families tend to live in cottages that are decorated with furniture that suits them best, along with the other decor mentioned earlier. The inside of Animalian houses have the furniture that people in Humania have as well, but a notable difference is that they do not use any type of technology. They would never use anything that could hurt the environment around them, such as harmful gasses or chemicals. Since nature blessed them with everything that they need, they use the resources provided to them to live a peaceful and quite interesting life. The volcano that forms the nose of the cat-shaped island, Mount Anaconda, has erupted. Many families who have gone to college in Humania still have the license ship to come to Humania *because of this incident. Nature has been hurt badly there..."*

I closed the page in shock, I had no idea that the humans knew this much about the eruption and Animalians. *I'll ask for my parents to buy me a laptop so I can research this author...*

I opened the title page of the book and checked the name of the author, Shannon B. I memorized the name when I suddenly bumped into the fountain in our front yard.

"OW!"

Moments later, Mom opened the door and spotted me. "Penelope! How was your day?"

"Oh, um, alright!" I responded, skipping over the threshold and into the house.

When Mom walked into the kitchen, I quickly slipped the book into my backpack. I joined her at the kitchen table, and I explained how my day went, leaving out the parts with Brandon and the two Animalian books.

10 minutes later, Clara barged into the house and threw her backpack against the wall of my dad's office area. "Hey."

"Clara, sweetie, how was your day?" Mom asked kindly.

"Good," she responded plainly.

Mom frowned. "Alright..."

Clara and Mom went to work preparing some chili for dinner, and Dad came home at five. We ate our dinner heartily, but Clara was scrolling through social media on her phone most of the time. Her phone case still had scorch marks on it, and she was always begging Mom and Dad to buy her a new one soon.

"Hey," I suddenly perked up, remembering my vow to ask my parents for my own personal laptop. "Could I have a computer all to myself?"

Mom and Dad exchanged glances.

"How about this," Mom said. "We'll get it for you next month. Until then, can you hang on?"

"I can," I assured her.

Later, I finished the homework Mrs. Firewood assigned us and brushed my teeth and combed my short black hair. I used a pet brush on my ears and tail and slipped on my Animalian nightdress with a fitting hole for my tail to slip through.

When Clara had fallen asleep in her bed with light blue bedsheets, I cracked open the next page of the book and shined a flashlight on the pages.

"*Animalian Culture and Clothing Items*

"*Animalians, just like their house options, wear clothing items that best suit their animal traits. For example, Animalians who have tails buy clothing from tailors and vendors that make sure to expertly leave a hole for their tails to slip through. There are even specific sizes for tails, just like Humanian measurements for clothing. Additionally, hats are also created for Animalians with large ear holes so they can comfortably look fashionable when they wear headwear.*

Moving on, many Animalians are vendors that sell antiques and unique items. They make their own block patterns and quilt the most beautiful pieces on the planet. Even rich Humanian buyers tend to purchase exotic items from Animalians."

I was getting sleepy, so I switched off the flashlight and closed the book. I pulled up the bedsheets and slipped the book under my bed. Then, I curled up into a ball and fell asleep.

***

I gasped when I realized that I was laying on the soft green grass back home at Animalia. I looked around my surroundings to get a glimpse of what was happening. I gulped for air, and I turned pale when I saw that a massive amount of smoke was swirling through the air. Mount Anaconda loomed in the distance, and my eyes widened when I recognized the ground under me was full of cracks that were filled with glowing red, hot lava. Before I could do anything, the earth shook, and I felt myself fall...and everything spiraled.

    My vision blurred as I fell, down, down to the earth. I gasped for air and saw myself sitting on the grass once again. I looked around me to see if I could recognize anything in my surroundings, but nothing seemed familiar. There was a small wooden hut just like mine back in Animalia, but this one was covered with climbing hydrangeas and mist flowers. There was a sparkling lake next to it and a field of cherry blossoms that lead to the outskirts of a forest.

Suddenly my eyes lingered on a cherry blossom tree close to the house and the shining lake. *A cherry blossom tree...Wait! I had heard a girl at the open house say something about cherry blossoms and a cottage...Hang on...is this the home of the girl who was talking to me?*

The dream dissolved before my eyes, and I sat up in bed, my face beaded with sweat. It was the middle of the night, and I tiptoed past Clara. I opened the curtains slightly and checked the clock on the wall. It read, 6:36 A.M.

*Oh, so it's already morning. Nothing like a fresh start...*I opened the bedroom door and walked slowly down the stairs. I grabbed my black backpack and walked into the kitchen. I was surprised to see my mother asleep on the small couch at the corner of the kitchen, wrapped in a blanket, with a cup of espresso in her hand.

"Mom?" I asked, taking a tentative step toward her.

She suddenly opened her right eye and got to her feet immediately when she realized it was me. "Oh, Penelope, you're already awake?"

"Yeah...I had a night terror," I explained. "Why aren't you in your bed?"

"I just needed to do some work last night," Mom explained. "Take out your breakfast, Penelope."

I grabbed some frozen waffles from the refrigerator and warmed them up in the toaster. When the *ding* sound erupted from the appliance, I whipped the waffles onto a dish and put heaps of maple syrup in the outline of a cat's head.

Mom finished her coffee and went to wash the dishes from last night. "Penelope?" she suddenly asked, placing the last glass cup in the dishwasher.

"Yes, Mom?" I asked through a mouthful of my sticky breakfast.

"I just wanted to let you know," Mom continued, "that I won't be able to drop you to school today. Nor will your father, he'll have to drop Clara early this morning because she has a special assembly for eighth graders today. You'll have to go by bus if that's alright with you."

"That's fine," I said, but my stomach tightened when I thought of Brandon being on the bus. "But why can't you drop me?"

"I have a job interview this morning. I want to work at the local bank, The Bank of Small Town."

"Oh," I said. "Yeah, that's fine. Good luck for the interview."

I finished my breakfast and got my lunch and snack ready. I packed my backpack and waved to Mom as I exited the house and began to walk to the bus stop, which was a few meters down the road from our house.

I pulled my hood over my face when I realized that Brandon was at the bus stop, goofing around again with his friends. I caught a glimpse of a page in that terrible book he was reading. There were many terrifying pictures of Animalians that were clearly faked.

Moments later, there was a huge *screech* as the bus pulled in beside the bus stop. I boarded and hurried to find a seat in the front, near the bus driver, and the bus began to drive the September Dawn.

***

As I walked into my classroom, the gears in my brain were turning as I thought about the girl, the hut, and the cherry blossom trees. Then, the voice of the girl suddenly flooded into my brain. My eyes widened. I had a good hunch about who it was.

Lilith was running late today, so I unpacked and waved to Jeremy. I unstacked the chairs at my table and sat down in my seat. As I worked on my morning work, Lilith burst into the classroom a few moments after the announcements had finished.

"Lilith?" I asked after she had unpacked and taken her seat behind my desk.

"Yeah?"

"Um, how do I put this…" I stuttered.

Lilith looked a bit confused. "What is it? You can ask me anything, I won't mind."

"Well," I said. "Were you that strange disappearing girl at the open house?"

Lilith seemed a bit surprised at my bluntness. "I-"

Jeremy interrupted, "A strange disappearing girl? That means there might be a person with magical abilities around here. The legend says that some people are given a gift from God, possibly earned in their past lives, and they sometimes get powers. Just like Animalians getting blessed by nature spirits."

"Oh, I see..." Lilith said, but I noticed that her face was as serene as ever. "Or it could just be someone playing a prank on you, right?"

I felt like she was hiding something. "I guess..."

"Penelope, can I tell you and Jeremy something after school...I'd rather not say it here," Lilith said uncomfortably, squirming in her seat.

"Yeah that's fine," I agreed, wondering what she had to say.

Jeremy nodded.

***

The Cat of Small Town

Mrs. Firewood told us to go to the bus loop near the garden, where Lilith, Jeremy, and I started to hang out for a bit during dismissal. Jeremy and I went on the same bus, which was always quite late, so we got to talk for a bit. Lilith usually walked home, but to where, I had no idea.

"So," I began, once we entered the garden with our backpacks slung over our shoulders. "What did you want to tell us, Lilith?"

"It's sort of a long story," she explained. "Let's sit down first."

We sat around the picnic table beside a huge weeping willow.

"Well," began Lilith. "It all started with my parents. They died when I was young, and my deer brother, Tasuke-"

"Wait, you have a brother?" Jeremy asked.

"Yes," said Lilith, a bit impatiently. "He's also a deer."

"WHAT?" I almost jumped out of my seat. "I thought you meant he was "dear" to you!"

"Well," Lilith said. "He is, but he's also a deer. Anyways, my parents lived in a pretty little hut...and I've been in that house ever since, hidden. Until a teacher during his lunch break from September Dawn found me, and he chased me because, well, I have to go to school. I followed him back to school after he gave up, and I came back during the open house when you found me. And then I kind of got myself found again so I could be taken to school by that counselor on the first day. So, yes, Penelope. I was the girl."

I looked at Lilith in shock. She had gone through all this?

"I am so sorry you had to go through all of that!" I suddenly remembered the cloudy mist that had blocked her from view that day. How had it been there? "Wait! There was a cloud of mist after you...puffed!"

Jeremy started laughing so hard after I said "puffed", and I joined him, but Lilith was looking at me with sad eyes. She seemed quite serious.

"So, um, after you disappeared there was a cloud of mist...How though? It was in the evening, and it wasn't humid at all..." I asked when we calmed down.

"Oh...I don't know how..." said Lilith, staring down at her shoes, but I could tell she was hiding something, *again*.

I figured I shouldn't ask more since she had told us one of the hardest things that had happened to her and realizing she had gone through all of those made me feel horrible. *While I may be having some lame struggles with bullies, she's going through much more...*

"I am sorry those things happened to you, Lilith...but I can't believe it! What happened to you is just like a fairy tale that I've read a lot of times," Jeremy pointed out, but I could tell he was genuine about feeling sorry for Lilith.

"Thanks a lot, guys," before Lilith could say anymore, the bell rang, and it was time to go home.

CHAPTER 6

When I arrived at my house, Mom was waiting for me inside the living room. She had changed out of her interview suit and was sitting down on the sofa and reading her book quietly. I hung my backpack on the coat rack and hugged her.

I was afraid to ask about the interview in case she hadn't gotten the job, but I managed to get the words out. "How did the interview go?"

Mom smiled, and I felt relieved. "The manager was quite rude, and he didn't want to give me the job because I was an Animalian, but his assistant was quite nice. I'll be working at the bank from now on!"

"I'm so happy for you, Mommy!" I exclaimed.

As I was about to run up to my room to read my library book, Mom said, "And Penelope?"

"Yes, Mom?" I turned.

"Expect your new laptop soon, if we're lucky."

The Cat of Small Town

***

The next few weeks whizzed by like a paper airplane soaring through the air. I did well in school and kept on renewing *The World of Half-Animals: Animalians and their Customs.*

    Then, one Friday, when I came back from school, Mom told me she had a surprise for me. I had completely forgotten about wanting a laptop since I had been so work-bound for the past five weeks, so I assumed Mom had bought Clara and me some new Animalian clothes.

    But as soon as Dad and Clara arrived home, Mom whipped out a sleek white box. *Laptop!* my brain screamed. Mom let me slide the cover off the box and a white laptop was tucked safely in the bubble wrap. I yelled in delight as I got to hold it, and Mom attached a violet computer cover that matched my eyes to the laptop.

    Clara let me borrow some of her stickers to plaster all over the cover, and soon the laptop was a masterpiece. Dad, who was the technology expert of the house, set the laptop up and I whispered a password into his ear.

After dinner, my laptop was all ready to go. I sprinted up to my room and grabbed my library book. I copied the name of the author, Shannon B., into the computer web browser, and a very short bio popped up in the search results.

I expected a picture of the author next to the bio, but in the profile box, there was just a default gray emoticon person. The bio read:

Shannon B. is a young reader's literature author, who has won multiple awards for her works. She writes both fiction and non-fiction books for young readers and has many fans. Some of her most popular books include The World of Half-Animals: Animalians and their Customs, The Lake of Hyacinths, *and* The Cherry Blossom Forest. *However, she has not shared her location as of yet, so her address remains a mystery.*

I clicked on the images section of the search results, but only Shannon B.'s books showed up. With a sigh, I shut my computer screen and lied down on my back.

I was startled by a knock at my door.

"Penelope, can I come in?" I heard my mom's voice float in from outside the door.

"Yeah," I said softly.

Mom slowly opened the door to my room. "It's almost 9 p.m. Penelope, you should go to sleep, or else it's going pass your bedtime," she said, raising one eyebrow at me.

Dang it! I had forgotten what time it was!

"Sorry, Mom, I just got too deep into my research. I'll go ahead and get ready to go to bed," I said, and quickly led her out of my room.

I slipped on my nightdress and jumped on to my bed. I lied down on the comfortable and soft bed sheets, and I quickly picked up my library book which I had hidden under my pillow when Mom came in. I couldn't stop thinking about Shannon B. and how she knew all about Animalians...

CHAPTER 7

A knock on my door made me jump from my bed and open my drowsy eyes. The door slowly opened with a crack.

"Ahh!" I yelled, while rubbing my eyelids and squinting in the sudden brightness of the room to see who it was.

It was Clara who was in her blue pajamas that had a cute white bunny pattern on them. "Sorry! Mom told me to wake you up because breakfast is ready. Also, can you please tidy up your room a bit? I have a sleepover today with my friends."

"Oh, okay, I'll clean my room later and I'll be downstairs for breakfast in a minute," I said, looking up at her cute pajamas, and her morning hair and wings.

Clara nodded and slowly closed my door and left. I could hear her footsteps become more and more muffled as she left the room and walked down the stairs.

When I came downstairs, I was greeted with a strange sight. Dad was wearing Mom's bright pink apron that was too tight for him, and I couldn't hold my giggles in as he flipped chocolate pancakes in the kitchen when I came downstairs.

"Morning!" I smiled.

"Morning!" Dad said.

Mom was sitting at the kitchen table, munching on some buttered bread. I frowned when I realized she was on her phone, texting her boss.

I started taking a bite out of two pancakes and slurped on some orange juice, and Clara had some Humanian cereal *without* milk.

When I pulled the cup out of my mouth, Clara burst into laughter at my orange mustache. "You look like-er-"

I quickly wiped the orange juice with the back of my hand. "Forget you saw that, Clara. Anyways, are you excited for your sleepover?"

"Of course I am."

After breakfast, we all readied our tiny home for Clara's friends to come over. Clara hid all my "baby" belongings because she would be embarrassed if her friends saw them. She also made sure her phone stood out so she could show it off to her friends.

The Cat of Small Town

***

At 6, the doorbell rang and a pretty girl with dark brown hair and striking black eyes entered the house. Her name was Lucia, one of Clara's weird friends. Then Tony, a tall dude that had a bright tan with blonde locks came a few minutes later, and Clara fussed over him when he entered the house. Sakurai was last to arrive, and she had baked some chocolate brownies for Clara. Sakurai had short, dark blue hair that was up to her ears and kind of spiky at the ends.

"I thought your sister was coming?" Clara inquired Sakurai.

"Yeah," Sakurai turned around. "She was right next to me while coming inside. I don't know where she is," Sakurai said, worried.

Suddenly, I sensed someone entering the house. A girl with a gentle smile, fair skin, rosy cheeks, and beautiful light blue hair flowing down her slender shoulders walked through the door. I immediately recognized her as Luxury Faimen, a girl in my class, who Felicia wanted to make her minion. I didn't talk to her much at school, but I wondered if I could be her friend.

"There you are!" Sakurai slung her hand around Luxury's neck.

Luxury's cloud blue eyes shined. "Sorry, sis, the wind outside is a bit extreme."

Clara led her friends into the kitchen, where Sakurai handed out the brownies. They were delicious, and I praised Clara's awesome friend.

Then, we ran upstairs with the other kids, but Clara went to show her friends her room, leaving Luxury and me in the upstairs loft. We sat down on the carpet for a few minutes in silence, until Luxury said, "I know we've been in school for six weeks, but we're in the same class, right?"

"Yeah, we are."

"Nice to see you out of September Dawn, then. I'm sorry that I haven't spoken to you in class. Felicia doesn't approve of me speaking to you at school, but I want to disobey her more and more. She kind of *forced* me to be her friend," explained Luxury.

"Oh," I said. "I guess so. You're right, though. You don't have to do what she says or let her make decisions for you."

Luxury nodded, and we were quiet for a little while longer, until Clara marched out of her room with Sakurai, Lucia, and Tony.

"We're going to watch a movie," she announced. "But it's for big kids, so you guys have to watch some baby shows instead."

"Oh," Luxury and I said in unison.

They all dashed downstairs and the teenagers went into the living room to watch their "big kid" movie. Luxury and I flicked on the television in the loft, and I asked her if she knew any good Humania movies we could watch.

"No, you can choose. I'd like to try Animalian ones," Luxury insisted.

"Oh well, I'll check if any of the channels have one," I said.

However, after minutes and minutes of scrolling through the TV channels, not a single Animalian movie was on. I gave up when a documentary on Channel 19 blared.

My eyes widened as I realized the narrator was narrating about Mount Anaconda's eruption. The camera zoomed in on a baby wolf Animalian, who was in ragged clothes, and was as thin as a toothpick. Her parents were nowhere in sight, and she was crying in the ruins of her hut.

My eyes flicked to the date of the documentary. It was from two months ago, when the volcano had first erupted.

"Oh...I never thought how much people suffered there in Animalia after the eruption!" Luxury said with genuine sadness.

"Yeah, I wish I was there to help," I said with tears in my eyes. "But I am here now, and it's not safe..."

"It's okay, Penelope! Don't hurt yourself from what happened in the past! Keep on going! The future is your destination! No turning back!" Luxury said, and she turned off the TV.

"You are right, Luxury, thank you!" I said, smiling at her.

"So, what should we do now-" Before she could continue her sentence, I smiled mischievously and hit her harshly with the pillow that was placed beside us on the couch we were sitting on.

"HEY!" she yelled, laughing and she ran for the other pillow on the couch.

When she reached for it, voices started coming up from the stairs.

"What are you guys doing?" said Clara, looking at me and Luxury as if she was a private investigator.

"Um-" I began.

"We were at a good part!" Lucia complained, flicking her dark locks over her shoulders. "The movie just became *so* dramatic-"

"Hush!" Sakurai chided. "They're too naive to understand anything."

Luxury snickered, and I stifled a giggle. Suddenly, Mom called everyone to the kitchen.

As we entered the kitchen, the aroma of mouthwatering Animalian delicacies filled the whole room, making me realize that I was starving. Everyone sat down around the kitchen table and Mom went around the circle, asking Clara's friends if they'd like to try some of the Animalian dishes she had prepared. Lucia rudely shook her head, Tony declined with slight disgust in his voice, and Sakurai politely refused.

Luxury was the only one beside me who would eat the dishes Mom had taken a lot of patience and thought to cook. (Clara, seeing as her friends did not want to try the food, decided to not eat either) I watched eagerly as she bit into the pistachio cake with avocado and whipped cream on the side on the plate just to make it healthier and the way Animalians like it!

I smiled as she said, "Yum! This cake is amazing! I've never tried Animalian food before. It's amazing! I wish there were some Animalian restaurants in town..."

Mom smiled, seeing that someone had eaten the cake that she had made. "Thank you! I am glad you like it," she said. "And you know, Luxury, maybe I could start one in the near future!"

Luxury smiled at her and looked at Tony, Lucia, and her sister Sakurai. "Do you guys want to eat it now? It's so delicious, and who knows, this could be our once in a lifetime opportunity to eat Animalian food! You guys know that, right?" She raised her eyebrows.

"No thanks," said Lucia in a disgusted tone.

"No thanks...I am good," said Tony, also in a rude way.

"I am not hungry right now, thank you. I am so sorry!" said Sakurai kindly.

At least someone is being kind while saying "no thank you", I thought. Still, it makes me angry with them for not appreciating how much Mom put work into the cake.

I stormed upstairs and snatched my book from my nightstand. However, I rushed back downstairs so I wouldn't come off as rude to everyone at the dinner table, especially Mom and Luxury.

Mom frowned. "Are you okay, Penelope? Why did you go upstairs?"

"Nothing," I lied. "Just needed my book."

Mom's amber eyes glanced at the cover. They widened when they lingered on the title.

"Penelope, where did you get this book?" she asked in a serious tone that made me feel uncomfortable.

"I-I got it from the school l-library," I said, shaking.

"Can I have a look at it later?" she asked, still staring at the book with a strange look on her face.

"O-of course!" I said, wondering why she was so serious and surprised about this unimportant book.

Thankfully, she didn't seem very frightened of it, only curious. I gulped as she opened it to the first page.

CHAPTER 8

That night, when everyone was sleeping, I kept on wondering and dreaming about why Mom looked that way when she saw the book.

When morning rolled around, my eyes stung from all the nightmares and how much I had woken up in the middle of the night, so since I didn't sleep for the amount of time that I must sleep every day to be energized for school, since the next day was a Monday.

After Clara's friends and Luxury left the house after breakfast, Mom started cleaning the house and asked us if we could clean our rooms to help her out. Clara and I nodded, and we went upstairs to our rooms. I took some disinfecting spray and a wet wipe and cleaned Clara's vanity which was overloaded with chip crumbs and cleaned my table since it was kind of dirty.

When we finished cleaning, I got myself ready for school, and I climbed into my father's car.

***

When I arrived at September Dawn Academy, I quickly ran inside the building. I rushed toward my classroom. The children in the hallways were like obstacles that were blocking the way to my destination. I ducked and dodged past them, and I finally made it to Mrs. Firewood's class.

    I slowly opened the door which gave a ferocious creak and was shocked to see that there were only six people inside the room. For the first time, Lilith was early and looking over a book with Jeremy at her desk. Of course, Brandon was at his desk, smirking at me, ready to shove the horrible library book in my face, but I chose to ignore him.

    Felicia was sketching in her notebook, and I winced at the sound of the lead being pressed hard in the paper. I narrowed my eyes at the page and realized she was drawing an ugly picture of me, and I looked like a monster. I averted my gaze, my eyes stinging.

    Thankfully, Luxury was there too, reading her book. She smiled at me, glancing up from her book, and I smiled back at her. Then, I quickly went up to Lilith and Jeremy to tell them all about Shannon B., and what had happened the day before. As I walked over to them, Lilith raised her head tentatively from the large book.

"Hi, Penelope! How are you?" she asked.

"Hey Penelope," said Jeremy, still reading the book that Lilith and he were looking at moments ago.

"Hi!" I spoke. "I'm okay, thanks! How are you?"

"I am okay," she said, but her tone didn't make me feel like she was lying.

"Jeremy, how did your weekend go?" I asked, trying to find a way to start to tell them about Shannon B. and the sleepover.

"It was good, I went to drink some bubble tea on Sunday, and visited the library to get 35 more books, since I finished the 40 books that I had gotten the day before," he said, as if getting more than 30 books and finishing them in one day was something people always did. When he glanced up, I think he noticed our shocked faces and reassured us, "I always do this...it's normal."

    I understood that he was trying to fix the awkwardness of the moment, but saying this just made it weirder.

    "Anyways," I said. "Well...um..."

    Lilith glanced over at my library book which was hanging out of my backpack. "Oh, is that your book?"

    Before I could say anything, she walked over to it and gently pulled it out. I could see that she curious, just like Mom had been.

    "This book has a lot of information about Animalia in it. I believe I have the exact same one at home! I think...my mom got it," she said.

    "Oh, I see." I looked at her with curiosity. "So, as I was going to say, this book's author...I want to meet her. She seems to know a lot about Animalia, and I wonder how, and why."

    "Penelope, you know that nobody knows where the author of this book lives?" Jeremy asked, still looking at his book. "Shannon B.'s an incredible author, and I'd like to meet her too, especially to get one of my favorite novels by her signed, but it seems impossible to do so."

"Yeah, you might be right," I said, but I still wondered how this author knew so much about Animalia. "I wish she had a fan mail account online at least..."

Lilith seemed to sense my disappointment. "It's...fine, I guess. So, Penelope, what did you do over the weekend?"

"Clara had a sleepover with her friends, so I had to clean some of the rooms in our house because they were *so* messy. But it also kind of gave me some time to just relax and be by myself. And when Clara's friends were off watching a movie, I actually just hung out with Clara's friend's little sister, Luxury! She was interesting to talk to-"

"Luxury, from our class? The girl who hangs out with Felicia...?" Jeremy asked, kind of serious and shocked.

I understood why he was acting this way. Felicia had been mean to us, and still was, but Luxury had said she didn't support her. I could tell that she wasn't lying to me that day.

"She doesn't support Felicia! Felicia tries to force her into her minion friend group, since she's really cool! She isn't like Felicia or Felicia's minions Simona and Verda!" I said, a bit louder than I wanted to.

Jeremy sighed, still looking seriously at me. "I'm going to ask Mrs. Firewood if I can go to the school library to return this," he said, raising the book in his hands.

Then, he quickly scuttled over to Mrs. Firewood's desk.

I frowned and looked over at Lilith for help, but all she did was shrug.

***

"How was your day?" Mom asked when I came through the door.

"It was fine, as always."

"I see,"

I grabbed my crumbled homework out of my backpack, which was some lame multiplication problems. I hightailed upstairs and jumped on my squishy bed and started to work on my homework. More than two times, I accidentally speared the paper all the way through with the tip of my extra-sharp mechanical pencil.

I placed the homework sheet back in my backpack when I finished, and by that time, Clara had already come home. I placed my ear to the door of her bedroom, and I heard her talking on the phone with one of her friends.

They were using funny slang and I stifled a laugh as I hightailed it out of there. I dashed into the kitchen where Mom was preparing some tomato soup, I could see that she was using a cheese grater on a special type of cheese from Animalia so we could sprinkle some on the soup to make it more delicious than it was already.

Dad arrived home at 7, which worried Mom. She laughed as he tried to drink the soup from the cooking spoon. I grinned happily, remembering the story of how Mom had met Dad.

Mom told me that when Dad was in his third year of college, for Christmas break, he went back to Animalia to visit. But when he went to the local mall for Christmas shopping, he met Mom, who was working as a staff member at a department store. Dad had seen Mom again the next week of Christmas break at his favorite coffee shop, and my mom told me that when they had walked in at the same time, the workers had thought that they were a couple and had given them matching espresso coffees.

    Mom said that they had laughed over the mix-up, and Dad and Mom had sat down across from each other at the same table. They eventually ended up going on multiple dates that Christmas break, and when Dad had to return for his final year in college, they kept in touch with letters. Eventually, they ended up getting married, and began to live a life together in Animalia. Then Clara and I came along...

***

The next day of school was not unlike any other, until Mrs. Firewood clapped her hands after lunch to get our attention. The class returned another three claps and fell silent.

"Class," Mrs. Firewood began. "I have a very, *very* important announcement to make. Well, it depends because you may find it important, or not."

"Get to the point!" I heard someone yell. With my razor-sharp hearing skills, I automatically knew it was Felicia.

Mrs. Firewood didn't seem ruffled. Instead she chuckled and said, "Alright, alright. Class, we'll be going on our first field trip this year, only next week. Jeremy, could you pass out the field trip forms for me? They are on my table,"

Jeremy rose and collected the forms that were on Mrs. Firewood's table. He went around the classroom, passing around the papers in his hands. When he slid a form towards me, I grabbed it and scanned it over. In Animalia, we'd had one field trip a year. I wondered what would be different in Humania this time...

The paper looked similar to the field trip forms in Animalia, except this form was much plainer. It simply stated all the precautions and details about the trip, without any images of the place.

"Oh...!" said Lilith from beside me. "We're going somewhere called the

Grapevine Mountains. Apparently, there are some cool museums up there and some camping stuff too."

As soon as Lilith mentioned a mountain, my stomach began to turn inside out.

I felt a bit queasy, and I replied in a small voice, "Cool."

As Jeremy returned to his seat in front of me, Lilith glanced sideways at me, like she knew something was wrong. But then she shook her head and turned back to her form.

CHAPTER 9

The rest of the school day passed by quickly. Lilith and Jeremy were kind of quiet, which made me uncomfortable, even though sometimes I liked some peace and quiet. When my bus was finally called, I quickly got my backpack and jacket and left the garden for the bus loop. Jeremy walked after me, but I felt bad for not saying "bye" to Lilith. I just wanted to go home so badly. When I walked onto the bus, I quickly found a seat close to front to avoid Brandon and his friends.

The bus was more crowded than usual. Jeremy slid into the seat next to me, and the bus drove out of the bus loop. Lilith waved from the garden, and I waved back slowly.

At the first stop, Jeremy asked, "Are you excited for the field trip?"

"Oh, um," I said, remembering that the class was going to a mountain. "Yeah."

Jeremy grinned. "Me too. I wonder if there'll be book butterflies there. I've only read about them, kind of like Animalians before I met you. Book butterflies are supposedly *very* rare to find, and even catch. They can only come to life from magic, specifically nature magic or air magic."

"Oh, cool."

"Yeah."

We were silent as the bus bumped to the next stop, but then I suddenly said, "Do you think Lilith is...a bit special? I don't know...she seems a bit mysterious, and on foggy days, the mist seems to bend towards her. Is it just me...?"

She had always been kind of mysterious in some way in my mind.

Jeremy shrugged, but he was serious. "I agree she's...unique. But I don't know for sure, Penelope."

The bus stopped at the third stop, Maple Breeze Street, where Jeremy waved and got off. I stared in silence out of the window after he had exited the bus.

***

I clutched the brown paper bag Mom had given me which contained my lunch, snack, water bottle, and smartwatch, just in case I needed to call her. The whole class stood in a line in the bus loop, waiting for our ride to arrive.

    Mrs. Firewood had hinted that the bus would be "fancy", whatever that meant, but as soon as the bus came rolling to a stop in front of us, everyone's jaws dropped to the floor. The bus was very long and was the color of sand. It had a beautiful blue pelican logo on it, and inside was even more glamorous. The seats were cushioned, and custom pink pillows were everywhere. There were little TVs on the back of the seats, and I hoped Mrs. Firewood would allow us to watch a movie. As we all got inside the bus, everyone started pushing and shoving, trying to save seats for their friends.

    The chaos didn't last for long, however, because Mrs. Firewood yelled, "I've assigned you with partners for this field trip! So, no pushing on the bus, please!"

    "Boo!" I heard someone yell.

    I looked around to see who it was, but thanks to my cat senses, I could see that it was one of Felicia's minions with green hair, hazel eyes, and a cruel smile, Verda.

Mrs. Firewood ignored Verda's rudeness. "Okay, so, Brandon, Zack and Simona you will be partners...Penelope, Felicia, and Jeremy!"

I stiffened. Lilith...she wasn't my partner for the trip. And Felicia? She would talk about how weird I was right to my face for the whole ride.

I glanced at Lilith and Jeremy. Jeremy was staring at Lilith. He looked a bit sad and annoyed. Lilith was standing in the aisle, not speaking, and looking at her baby blue backpack with a star and flower sticker on it, which she had gotten a special exception to have by the counselor who took her to school that first day.

"For our last group, Luxury and Lilith! Alright everyone, we'll be going in a second. I'll give everyone somewhere to sit with their partners," said Mrs. Firewood.

She showed all of us our assigned seats. To our luck, Luxury and Lilith sat across the aisle from us.

I made a move for the window, since it had the nicest view of the landscape as we drove. But Felicia's ice-cold hands found my uniform skirt, and she pushed me away.

She slid against the window, smirking. "Hey, Cat Freak, too bad. The *animals* don't have the luxury to take a trip. They have to stay alone at home with a mean old pet sitter, don't they, Verda?"

Felicia's minion cackled from the seat in front of us. "Well, I'll be sitting next to the window. And Book Nerd, you can sit far away from me. Cat Freak will be in the middle," she continued.

Jeremy quietly took his place next to me. I suspected he was used to being bullied and teased in this way. I looked over at Lilith. Her face resembled a misty morning, but she smiled warmly at us when she noticed that we were staring at her.

***

Felicia gossiped with Verda throughout the drive. However, I could barely say anything, as I was squished in the middle. Jeremy, like the gentleman he was, scooted over so his feet were in the aisle as much as he could to give me space. The seats, as fancy and as cushioned as they were, didn't stretch long enough to fit two like-minded people and a Felicia.

She wouldn't let my shoulders come six inches from hers, and if they did, she would harshly knock her elbow into me, leaving me with a sore side for the entire trip. I still got to join Jeremy and Lilith's conversations even though it was difficult.

The ride was a whopping two hours, and I struggled to stay in the position I was stuck in. However, getting glimpses of the landscape here and there was surely worth the discomfort. As the bus rolled down the road, the rolling hills of Humania and the huge sunflower fields took my breath away. Since it was still fall, the trees had turned into flames, their leaves floating down from the branches like ashes.

Finally, blue mountains towered my vision. *Oh, how majestic they are!* I though, excited. All the queasiness and discomfort vanished in an instant. I seemed to forget all about Mount Anaconda's eruption and took in the moment. Suddenly, I caught a glimpse of a girl in purple galloping at the speed of light on a glowing horse. A pure white squirrel sat squarely on her shoulder. As instantly as they'd appeared, they vanished.

I rubbed my eyes. *The light is playing tricks on me.* I glanced back up at the huge landforms in the distance. The mountains were a considerable five miles away at the least, and the bus was still rolling down a road in a flat field toward them.

Suddenly, the ground boomed. The world turned to the right, then to the left. I screamed as the mirror next to Felicia shattered, impaling the bully in multiple places. Jeremy fell sideways into the aisle, his glasses tumbling to the carpeted floor. As gravity took me into the aisle as well, I caught a glimpse of Lilith.

She was the only kid standing up without holding on to anything. She bit her lower lip, and her foggy eyes were in complete concentration. Her hands were slightly out in front of her, and something almost invisible, light air, seemed to be coming from her palms. The bus almost seemed to right itself, but I couldn't understand anything at the moment.

Another trick of the light. I shook my head, which bonked into the seat next to me. Jeremy was sliding forward down the aisle, trying to grab his glasses. My tail smashed against something unpleasant, and a shard of glass embedded itself in my hand.

    I had no idea where I was now, as everything had turned into nasty shades of brown, gray, and red. Then, just as I saw Luxury fly out a window, the tornado engulfed everything in black. I heard a scream in the darkness and I felt myself fly into the air just like that day two months ago.

CHAPTER 10

My eyes flickered open and shut as my vision cleared. I felt the spiky, frost-covered grass prickling my back. My limbs were tingling in the same way my funny bone would sting if I banged it against something.

I tried to stand up, but the pain pushed me down. I could see Lilith and Jeremy crawling on all fours towards me two feet away. They seemed to be in pain as well. Behind them there was a shadow of a woman standing on a frosted hill. I tried to take deep breaths in the crisp, cold air, but my lungs stung every time.

I took in the woman, but she was quite blurry. She was wearing a thick coat that wasn't completely closed and a scarf and she wore a brown sweater that had an image of a quill and ink on it.

"Penelope!" I heard Lilith yell, and then I hit the ground once again.

***

I woke up on a brown leather couch. There was a cup of hot lemon tea on the coffee table next to me, and a knitted red quilt was placed over my body. There was a wet cloth on my forehead, and when I tried to move my left arm, I realized a cloth made of tree leaves was wrapped around my palm where the glass had pierced me.

I guessed I was lying in a living room, since there were two armchairs beside the couch and a cozy fireplace was lit. I realized that Jeremy and Lilith were also wrapped in blankets, and they were sitting in the armchairs beside me. I glanced above the couch, where a window looked out to the valley beneath the mountains. *This house is built on the side of the mountains, isn't it?*

I sat up and the quilt slid off me. Jeremy and Lilith looked at me in surprise and joy.

"You're awake!" Lilith threw her quilt off her and jumped from her chair. She winced in pain, but she hobbled toward me and embraced me.

"Yeah," I said, still a bit dizzy. "One question...where are we?"

"Good thing you asked that," said a foreign voice from an opening in the wall that led to a kitchen area.

A woman about 30 years old walked inside the room. The stranger had straight black hair and blueish eyes with hazel highlights behind black circle glasses. Her shirt was the same as the woman I had seen earlier on the hill. She wore a silver locket around her neck, and I glanced to the entrance of the house, where a coat hanger stood. The same thick jacket was hung up on one of the arms.

"Penelope, this is…er, Miss S, who saved us…" said Jeremy.

"Hello, there. I'm glad you've come to. If you don't mind, I'll bring you guys some croissants with melted chocolate inside. Also, some homemade healing cream for your wounds," the woman called Miss S said.

"Thank you," Lilith said as the woman left the room.

"So, what happened…?" I asked.

The question had been circling in my head for too long.

Lilith sighed. "Well, um, so there was a tornado."

Jeremey whispered, "She probably already knows that."

"We don't know that...But um, well, we all went flying and we, um, landed at the base of the mountain, kind of safely because..."

Jeremy added, "And then Miss S found us and took us up the mountain. And well, that's it."

"Yeah..." Lilith said.

"How did we land safely? We should have broken every bone in our bodies! How are we even alive?!" I exclaimed.

"I-um...kind of landed us...? With, um, a parachute...?" Lilith said slowly.

I could tell she was lying.

I was about to respond, but Miss S came inside the room with a tray of fresh baked chocolate croissants and a warm but grim expression on her face. "The croissants are ready!"

I glanced behind her. At the dining table, there was only one tiny little chair pushed in at it. *I guess she's not used to having company*, I assumed. Then, I noticed some newspapers on the table. I squinted at them, trying to read what they said. The big title caught my eye. It read, "Where is Shannon B., Famous Kids' Author?"

Shannon B.! I realized. *All of the newspapers mention her...* I glanced up at Miss S. Everything on the table was about my favorite author. *I wonder...*

Suddenly there was a pound on the door, and the sound of a body thudding to the ground. Miss S' eyebrows furrowed in concern and maybe even annoyance. She peeked one blue eye through the peephole in her door. Miss S bit her lower lip, set the tray down, and reached for the doorknob.

I remembered that Shannon B. was known for staying mysterious. I connected the dots for Lilith as well. I glanced at my friend. I had gotten to know her and Jeremy so well that I didn't have to say anything for her to understand.

Lilith magically conjured a huge cloud of mist, which wrapped itself around Miss S, also known as Shannon B. I could barely see the author's form, but I could tell she was still there. Shannon turned to Lilith and gave her a grateful smile. She knew as well as Jeremy and me that Lilith had magical powers.

Lilith's eyes began to turn more of a misty and light color, and her hair was as white as snow as she used her magic. I watched in amazement as her hair instantly returned to its normal color and her eyes became that slightly darker blue color once again. Jeremy and I stared at her in shock and amazement. I could see that she was slightly embarrassed.

The door flew open. Our classmates dashed in, some of them mildly wounded, but most seemed alright. I gasped as Mrs. Firewood and the bus driver, looking exhausted, ran into the cottage, carrying a very injured Luxury on a makeshift pine tree bark stretcher. Blood clotted her light blue hair, and a nasty, large cut dripped red from her chest. Her eyes were closed, but I could see them moving rapidly under her eyelids. There were several shards of glass embedded in her face, and I winced as they laid her down on the couch.

No one seemed to notice Shannon B., who immediately fetched more casts, band-aids, and herbal creams. She handed them to Jeremy, who immediately knew what to do. I watched, holding my breath, as Luxury's breathing became slower and shallow. I checked her pulse. It was weak. My classmate was on the verge of death, and there was barely anything I could do.

Jeremy got right to work, and after an uncomfortable and tearful hour later, Luxury recovered gradually. She curled into a ball and fell into a deep sleep. Jeremy, Lilith, and I all looked at each other with joy.

Suddenly, Mrs. Firewood embraced us in a huge hug. I was surprised as she began to sob uncontrollably. I looked up at Mrs. Firewood's face. She seemed relatively okay, but her glasses had been broken like Jeremy's.

"Is...everybody alright...?" I asked the question, even though I knew it was hard to answer.

"Well..." said Mrs. Firewood, her forehead creasing. "We had a loss...Simona..."

She broke down in tears again, and I stared into space at the thought of Simona Rayband dying...

"Everyone and everything will be alright, believe me, Penelope. We just need a way to communicate with someone..."

Lilith cut in, pulling me away from Mrs. Firewood, who needed time to recover.

"Wait!" said Felicia, who had multiple small cuts on her arms from the window that had shattered on her. "I found Cat Freak-I mean, Penelope's lunch bag under the ruins of the bus. Didn't you bring a watch inside?"

She held the crumpled brown bag at her arm's length, like something disgusting was inside of it. *Of course! How could I have forgotten! Mom had packed up my bag and had given me a smartwatch to check in with me!*

I quickly snatched my bag from Felicia and opened it as fast I could. I looked down at it, then dipped my hand inside of it, careful in case shards of glass were inside. Finally, my hands touched something that felt like a cold screen that had almost been destroyed. I pulled it out, hoping that it was my watch.

As the item revealed itself in my hands, I beamed when I saw it was just what we needed. But its screen was close to being completely ruined. Everyone in the room was staring at me and my watch.

"I hope it works," I heard someone say from the crowd surrounding me inside the cottage.

"Yeah..." I took a deep breath and prayed it would work as I clicked on the power button on the right side of the watch to turn it on.

As the screen lit up, everyone in the room let out a cheer of joy. They crowded around me, trying to see their last hope of communication. I squinted at the blurry screen and clicked on the call button next to my mom's image in the calling section.

The call quickly opened, and I could see Mom's worried face. She was probably wondering why I hadn't come home yet from school and the field trip. But her worries only piled up more and more when she looked me over from head to toe, noticing the cuts on my face and my messy fur at my ears and hair.

"PENELOPE! ARE YOU OKAY? WHY ARE YOU-WHAT HAPPENED?" I saw her eyes dart towards the crowd behind me. Her eyes widened as big as saucers. "Where is your teacher? *What happened?*"

"Mom! Er...Everything is okay...but...um..." No words were able to come out of my mouth.

I turned to look at Jeremy and Lilith, but Lilith was confused and I could see that the cut on one of her legs was bleeding rapidly. I turned back to the watch. "There was a tornado, Mom. We're all safe in a house in the mountains, but you need to tell the school! Find someone to rescue us!" My eyes skipped across my classmates. "Some of us are wounded, Mom. Please, inform the school, the fire station!"

Suddenly, a notification appeared at the top of the cracked screen.

"Mom, do you understand? There's only 2 percent left in the watch!" I said.

Mom was silent for a second. "Alright, honey. Best not to waste words. I-I love-"

The watch died before she could finish her sentence. I gulped and turned to Lilith. I grabbed her gently by the arm and made her sit down in an armchair. Almost-invisible Shannon B. walked over to us and handed me a cast and gauze pad. I washed Lilith's cuts thoroughly and wrapped a cast securely around her leg. Jeremy was kneeling at the other armchair, attending to Brandon, when everyone suddenly stared at me. I realized that Lilith was somewhere else now, and I was attending to Ivan. I had already helped five other classmates without me realizing it.

"Wow, you sure work fast," said a recovered Luxury. She sat up on the couch and watched as I placed a band-aid squarely on Ivan's knee.

"You're awake!" I exclaimed, as Ivan hobbled out of the chair.

Luxury smiled. "I sure am. All thanks to you and your friends."

After everyone had been attended to, I stared out of the window that looked down from the mountain. The sun was setting and help still hadn't arrived yet. I called Shannon B. to my side, and my classmates raised their eyebrows since it seemed like I was talking to the air.

"You're Shannon B., right?" I whisper-asked her.

She sighed. "Yes, that's correct. I assume you knew from the newspapers over there?"

"Yeah..." I stared at my feet. "Is there any way you can help us get home? And also...in one of your books...*Animalians and their Customs: The World of Half Animals*...I was wondering how you knew so much about us...about me."

Shannon sighed again. "For your first question, I...I don't have any way of speaking to the outside world. Pretty dumb, huh? Well, in my defense, it's not every day that a tornado comes rolling around in the valley and some fifth graders get injured and stuck here...And about the Animalian thing...well-"

My face darkened, and I interrupted her. "Is that so? Well, HOW ARE WE SUPPOSED TO GET OUT NOW, HUH?"

I began to cry. Everyone was staring at me in shock, but I couldn't even *think* about being embarrassed. In my mind, I felt myself falling through the earth, Mount Anaconda in the distance, lava everywhere. Everyone I cared about was shrieking as they were sucked up into the cracks in the earth. I was falling, falling, falling down a dark pit in the ground that had no end. I squeezed my eyes shut.

Suddenly, arms upon arms wrapped around my shoulders, engulfing me with warmth. I felt myself being lifted, out of the earth and into the fluffy clouds. I opened my eyes. My classmates were all embracing me, even Felicia, Verda, and Brandon. I could see and feel Mrs. Firewood join in too. That must have been the warmth I felt.

They slowly removed their arms from my shoulders, and Lilith gingerly patted me on the back. "Thank you for supporting all of us through this disaster. It's hard to be strong like that. Now, it's our duty to support you." She smiled warmly.

Jeremy said, "You're amazing, Penelope. You really are."

My face reddened under my friends' gazes. "Thanks, you guys. No, you're the amazing ones."

We hugged, and I was so grateful that my friends were there to support me. Shannon B. suddenly appeared next to us as we broke apart.

"You didn't answer my question," I reminded her.

She nodded. "I assume I can trust you."

"To the death," I said confidently, but when Lilith and Jeremy looked confused, and Shannon raised her eyebrows, my face burned with embarrassment. "Nevermind. I mean, you can trust me."

"You see, my mother was an Animalian. My father was from Humania. This was the first time the two species mixed. Usually, Animalians only go to college in Humania, and Humanians only tour Animalia as visitors. But my parents married secretly and stayed here, in the mountains. I grew up here as well. I still have Animalian traits, though. I hibernate in the winter after completing a book, and when I wake up in the spring, I publish it."

"So, you are kind of like a bear?" asked Jeremy, looking in the wrong direction, facing behind us, since his glasses were broken. I giggled.

"Jeremy...she is in front of us...not behind..." I heard Lilith whisper to Jeremy.

Jeremy quickly turned around to face Shannon B., in the right direction this time. He looked kind of embarrassed.

"Yes, I have the traits of a bear," Shannon B continued. "I have an agent in Animalia who informed me about Mount Anaconda, if you're wondering."

"Oh, I see..." I said softly.

"It's almost nighttime. You can ask your classmates and teacher if they would like to stay here for the night. I have some comfortable sleeping bags and mats they can lay on for the night," Shannon B. said, pointing at the window, where I saw the beautiful sky filled with stars and the black color of the night sky dripping on top of gradually disappearing layer of yellowish orange.

We all nodded. "I don't think we have any other choice."

***

I had finally fallen asleep after a long and painful day, but a whisper startled me, causing me to wake up.

"Penelope, it's me, Shannon. please go wake up Lilith please, I think your friend Jeremy is already awake," said the voice.

"Huh? Why-what's going on?" I sat up in the sleeping bag.

As my vision cleared, Shannon B. vanished. I slipped out of the sleeping bag and looked around, trying to spot the couch where Lilith was offered to sleep on in the dark. Since cats had excellent night vision, my eyes found the couch easily. I could see that a lot of kids in my class were sleeping on the carpet that was next to it. *What am I supposed to do now?* I wondered.

"Psst, Penelope, what are you doing?" asked a voice behind me.

My hair and fur stood on end. I knew I shouldn't be scared of monsters in the dark, but I couldn't help myself from being frightened. I could barely sense the presence behind me.

"AHH!" I screamed, whipping around to see who it was.

I couldn't stop myself from shrieking.

"Woah! Calm down! It's me, Lilith!" said the dark figure in front of me.

"Lilith?" I asked, trying to make sure it wasn't any kind of monster.

"Yeah? Penelope, thankfully, no one woke up after you screamed. Also, I'm so sorry for startling you. I didn't mean to do that," Lilith said.

"It's alright," I said.

Shannon B. was in the kitchen, leaning against the wall with Jeremy beside her. Shannon was munching on a delicious-looking sandwich, which she put down as Lilith and I entered the room.

"So..." I began. "What did you want to talk about, Miss B.?"

Shannon cleared her throat. "You asked me earlier about Animalia, and my book. Well, I just wanted to make a connection here. Lilith, ever since you walked through the door, I couldn't help but think you reminded me of someone I knew...my sister-in-law, Sakura, and my brother, her husband, Caleb."

Lilith's eyes widened. I wondered what Shannon B. was talking about, but I was sure it was about the connection between the two of them.

"I also remember," said Shannon, "that I met you when you were only a baby. Sakura had named you Lilith, and when you arrived, that confirmed my thoughts. Do you still live in that quaint little cottage by the cherry blossoms and that foggy lake?"

Lilith nodded, but her eyes were still wide. "I do...but *what* is this about anyways?"

Shannon sighed. "I meant to say...that I am your aunt. Your father's older sister."

Lilith stumbled back a few steps, and almost tripped because of her injury. Before she could get more injured, I caught her arm, preventing her from falling. We both turned around to face Shannon. I was still shocked by what the author had said. She was Lilith's aunt?

"Wait," Jeremy cut in. "*You're* Lilith's aunt?"

Shannon nodded grimly. "Lilith, you are my kin, and I sense you will play a great part in the fate of the world with your friends. I have something to give you all."

Shannon signaled to follow her up a ladder at the back of the kitchen I initially thought was only for display. We climbed up, one by one, and entered a tiny little attic. Boxes filled with dusty books and random objects were everywhere. I bumped into the short ceiling, and narrowly avoided a cobweb.

Shannon crawled to the back of the attic and fished through a large box. Suddenly, she pulled her hand out. In her palms was a strange looking map that showed repeated images of a puddle, and there were dotted lines that showed different locations the puddle was at.

"Take this," said the author. "This map belonged to Captain Beasely himself. I inherited it from my father, who was a descendant of the captain. The "B" in my name stands for "Beasely"."

Jeremy's eyes widened even more than Lilith's. He walked up to Shannon and inspected the map.

"So, you mean *the* Captain Beasely? The guy who found Animalia centuries ago?" Jeremy asked as he scanned the map even more.

Shannon nodded.

Captain Beasely was the one who had found Animalia...from Shannon's book. No one taught us that in Animalia, but since Shannon is his descendant, she knew, and included it in her book...but, why is she giving us a map?

"Why are you giving it to us?" I asked aloud, even though she had already explained.

"You will play a great part in the world," she repeated. "And I-"

Suddenly, my ears picked up a faraway *whirr* sound. *Is it-?* I ran to the window.

I squinted at the dark sky, and I spotted two bright yellow helicopters circling the area. "GUYS!" I screamed. "HELP IS HERE! Everyone, come on! We need to find a way to let them know we're here!"

Everyone in the living room sluggishly got up, and as soon as they realized what was happening, they hustled to pack everything they had left from the incident. Thankfully, my mom had checked my location on the watch when I had called her.

I shuddered to think what would have happened if she hadn't. I looked at Lilith, and I watched as she pushed her messy hair out of her eyes, which reminded me that I hadn't taken care of my appearance either. I smiled as Lilith hugged her aunt, Shannon B., which had surprised me so much.

I looked over at Jeremy. He grinned at us. As Lilith broke her hug with Shannon, everyone quickly rushed outside with our classmates, the bus driver, and Mrs. Firewood. I started waving and yelling as loud as I could at the helicopter, trying to get the pilots' attention.

Suddenly, Shannon stepped outside. She threw her head back and let out a ferocious roar that could have been heard from miles away. I glanced around, just in case a *real* bear was around. The helicopters turned so they faced our direction, and they hovered for a few minutes directly above us.

Tears of joy streamed down my face as my eyes reflected the shiny silver landing legs of the helicopters. As soon as they landed, my classmates sprinted to them as fast as they could. A woman in the rescue squad uniform helped everyone up and inside safely.

I glanced around for my friends. Lilith was next to me, and I grabbed her hand. Luxury held on to Lilith's other arm, and Jeremy held mine on the other side. Together, we stepped onto the second helicopter, and another lady gave us a hand and securely strapped us in our seats. I was closest to the opening in the helicopter, and I waved at Shannon B. as we ascended into the sky and the mountains became smaller every second.

CHAPTER 11

Since the hospital closest to the mountain was full, the pilot announced we would arrive back in Small Town in an hour. I was grateful that it wasn't two hours, as helicopters traveled faster than buses.

During the trip, I held hands with Lilith, who kept wincing every now and then. I could tell, even with the cast and tea, the deep cut on her leg still pained her. I wanted to cry. I realized that when the tornado had first hit, Lilith tried to command the air and clouds around her to righten the bus, but in the process of doing so, a huge metal chunk had slashed her leg badly.

I squeezed her hand, and I tried to make her forget her pain for just a little bit. "We'll be there soon!" I whispered in her ear.

Lilith returned a slightly pained smile, but I could tell she was grateful for the support. I put my head back on the head cushion and closed my eyes. I gently slid my hands out of Lilith's and fell into a deep sleep.

∗∗∗

My eyes snapped open. The sound of seatbelts being unbuckled had woken me up. The helicopters landed on two helipads on the roof of September Dawn Public Hospital. Paramedics flooded to the roof, and even some people who seemed familiar. There were many adults who resembled some of my classmates.

A sharp-faced woman who had the exact same face as Felicia sprinted toward the other helicopter that Felicia exited, I assumed the woman was her mom, I watched as she pinched her ear. "HOW DARE YOU BE A FOLLOWER! WHAT DID I TELL YOU ABOUT THAT CAT GIRL?" she screamed.

Felicia looked like she was on the verge of tears, but she followed her mother and a nurse downstairs from the roof. Suddenly, as I got down from the helicopter, someone entered my line of sight. Long blonde hair. A swishy, fluffy yellow fox tail. Gentle blue eyes that were filled with newfound worry. The instructions a nurse was speaking to me suddenly muted in my brain. The only thing I could think about was being in my mother's arms again.

    I jumped into her chest, and she spun me around and around. Her face was shining, and I hoped mine was too. Mom placed me down gently. A light drizzle had started, and it was about three in the morning. I glanced behind me. Lilith was slowly descending the steps of the helicopter, and when the rescue squad woman asked if she needed help getting down, she refused and said she was fine. I left my mother's side to run up to her.

    Lilith was only a few feet away, and she hobbled toward me. Suddenly, the world slowed down. Lilith stumbled and cried out. Her leg couldn't support her weight anymore. She collapsed. I stopped in my tracks. I couldn't take all of this pain anymore. It seemed that wherever *I* went, the people I cared about got hurt.

    "LILITH!" I screamed.

    Luxury reached a weak hand out for my friend, but she was wheeled away in a wheelchair. I sprinted toward Lilith, nothing else in my mind except making sure she was alright. Jeremy, who had just gotten out of the helicopter, glanced in our direction. He froze for a moment, then, like the amazing friend he was, he snatched a stretcher from a shocked nurse and dashed to Lilith's side. Mom was also frozen in place. Her mouth was wide open, and her gaze lay on Lilith's unconscious body lying on the roof.

 I lifted Lilith into the stretcher, but the nurses pushed us out of the way and rushed downstairs. I stared after them, even after they had disappeared from sight. I might've stood there for over an hour if Jeremy hadn't led me away.

 Mom, Jeremy, and I all waited in the waiting room of the hospital. Brandon was there too with his mother, as chubby as him, as he was the only other person who wasn't heavily injured. I squeezed my mother's hand in worry, waiting for a nurse to allow us to see Lilith. Lilith had no family members who could take care of her at the moment, so we were the only people she had.

After over an hour, I asked Jeremy, "I was just wondering...where are *your* parents?"

After he didn't reply for a few moments, I immediately regretted asking him about it. But after a minute had passed he said, "Well...my parents...aren't involved in my life. They never remind me to do my homework or help me study for a test. For all I know, they're probably in their offices at home, writing a report for their bosses on their computers. They haven't even realized I'm not home, and they probably won't." He looked down at his dirty black school sneakers.

My eyes widened, then softened. "I know "sorries" aren't enough," I said. "All I want to say is: you've been so brave. It's hard to be independent like that for a long time."

Jeremy looked up at me and smiled. Then, he furrowed his eyebrows. "Penelope, I've been wanting to tell you-"

Just then, a beaming, brown-haired nurse entered the waiting room. "Lilith has recovered immensely. The cut on her leg has been properly treated, and I dare say, that cast helped her quite a bit."

"She's alright?" I hopped up from my seat. "C-can we see her?"

The nurse smiled. "Of course. Does she have any family-"

"No," I said quickly. "Please, show us where she is."

The woman nodded. "Follow me!"

I glanced at Mom. She was on the phone with Dad, but she nodded, allowing me to go ahead.

***

We found Lilith lying in her hospital bed, but she was wide awake. When she saw us, she sat up in bed, and another nurse chided the one who led us to Lilith for not letting our friend get rest.

I hugged Lilith tightly. "I'm so glad you're alright."

Lilith smiled and held me at arm's length as she spoke to me. "Really, I'm so embarrassed that I collapsed like that. But I'm so glad everyone's alright."

"Well..." said Jeremy, ruining the joyful mood. "Not everyone. Remember...? Mrs. Firewood mentioned one of Felicia's friends...Simona..."

"Oh yeah..." I said guiltily, even though there was no way we could have saved her.

"If I had been able to keep the bus from falling over..." Lilith said, tears in her eyes.

"It's not your fault, Lilith. You actually did a pretty good job keeping the bus from hurting anyone, even if for a little bit!" said Jeremy.

I nodded. Jeremy was right. Lilith was so brave to do that. If she hadn't, we all would have died just like Simona Rayband.

"Thank you so much, guys. I also still can't believe it...Aunt- Shannon B. is my aunt..." Lilith said, smiling. "She's my father's sister..."

"Me too, I would have never thought *anything* like this would happen," I said. "For some reason, disasters always happen when I go near mountains...I won't dare to go near one *ever* again."

"Don't say that!" laughed Lilith. "You'll have a wonderful experience on a mountain, I assure you!"

"Hey," Jeremy said. "That gave me an idea! How about, some time, we go apple picking at the mountain on the opposite side of town?"

"That's a great idea," I assured him. "But maybe later. I've had my fair share of mountains for today, at least."

We had a hearty laugh over it. Thankfully, Lilith was excused at seven thirty in the morning from the hospital. Lilith had healed completely, but Luxury had to be pushed around in a wheelchair for a few days at the least.

Clara and Dad arrived at the hospital at eight since the thunderstorm was relentless throughout the early morning. I remember Clara bolting into the lobby, bumping into the walls as she ran to me. At the time, I was pushing Luxury outside of the hospital with Jeremy, Lilith, and Mom, and when I saw Clara, I let go of the wheelchair handles and leaped into my sister's arms. She was crying uncontrollably, and I wiped her tears when we broke apart.

"I-I thought you were dead," she sniffled.

I laughed. "Oh, Clara, Clara, Clara. I've gone face-to-face with death *multiple* times. Didn't you think I could manage this time?"

Clara didn't answer. Instead, she broke down crying again. Dad appeared behind her, sweating from running from the parking lot and into the hospital. He wrapped Clara and me in a huge bear hug. Mom joined us, and we stayed there for a few moments.

My eyes glanced at Lilith, Jeremy, and Luxury who were awkwardly looking around the lobby as we stood there. I couldn't imagine being like Lilith or Jeremy: without a family that could support you. My family was my lifeline. We'd been through thick and thin, and we would stick together until the end of time.

As we broke apart, Luxury's parents and her sister Sakurai came a few minutes later. They had an emotional reunion as well. Soon, we waved goodbye to Luxury as she was wheeled back home by her family. Lilith waved goodbye soon after. She knew how to get home herself, she did some signal with her hands, and all I could see left of her was a faded figure that was hidden in the mist and fog. My family offered Jeremy a ride home, but he refused, saying he could make it home alone as well.

During the car ride back to our little house, everyone was quiet. Suddenly, Mom broke the silence by starting my favorite song on the radio. I swayed in my seat to the tune, and soon I got lost in it. I couldn't wish for anything more. I was just grateful that I got to live another day with my parents, friends, sister, and teacher at my side.

CHAPTER 12

I've gone to my mother's mom's funeral once in Animalia. It was the hottest day in Animalia, the day she died. It was before the eruption. Animalia had the biggest forest fire I had ever seen. Granny had tried to save a music box, but before she could even touch it, her home was set on fire. She had told me that the music box contained a flamingo Animalian ballet dancer which I would have loved to see.

However, here in a class full of people, it stressed me out more than ever. Humanian funerals were much more different from my own country's funerals. In Animalia, we would sing a song about how we appreciated our deity, Calla, the goddess of nature for the blessing she had given our ancestor long ago, a blessing for life.

And how grateful we were that the person who had left the earth had been in our lives. Then, a magical light would separate their soul, one piece of it growing into a flower to honor Calla, and the other, becoming a full animal. Granny had turned into a bright pink geranium, but I had raised my eyebrows when a turtle hadn't appeared. I'd always hoped I would meet someone with Granny's soul before I died myself.

September Dawn had given a week off for our class since we'd been through a *very* traumatic experience. After the week off had finished, everyone reentered the classroom. As soon as my shoes stepped on the floor of the classroom, I realized there was a picture of Simona on the back table. It had bright vermillion flowers wreathed around it, and many of my classmates had written notes for her soul. The notes were stacked in a pile next to her picture.

Simona's face was serious as usual, and her short red hair looked perfectly combed. Her golden and reddish eyes were sparkling with a slightly cruel light. Her shoulders were barely seen at the bottom, but they were very wide. Simona was known as the most dangerous of Felicia's minions, as she was the best soccer and football player at school, and everyone called her the "Red Jock".

A gentle hand with many beautiful silver rings touched my shoulder from my right side. "Penelope, come on inside, don't just stand there in the doorway. Don't worry, we're going to have a short class funeral for Simona. If you feel you want to write something nice for her soul to read, go ahead," said Mrs. Firewood.

I nodded, but I hadn't decided yet if I wanted to or not.

After I unpacked, I said "good morning" to Lilith, Luxury, and Jeremy. They all seemed back to normal, and I was glad.

"How was your week off?" I asked Lilith.

"It was good, I guess. I reread all of the books in my mother's small library," she responded.

"Sweet! By the way, are you excited for The Day of Spook? It's coming up just next week."

The Day of Spook was a popular holiday. We used to celebrate it in Animalia too. Basically, one night each October, kids got the chance to dress up in spooky costumes and go door-to-door, asking the inhabitants of the houses for treats. I didn't think a Humanian Day of Spook would be any different from how I used to celebrate it in Animalia.

"I am! I'm going to be a mystical witch or a mystical elf," Lilith explained. "I can't choose between the two, though!"

I smiled. "How about you be a...mystical witch with foggy powers?"

Lilith glanced around the room in case anyone was listening, but they were all chatting, crying over Simona, or reading a book. "You know, Penelope, that idea isn't half bad."

Later that day, we had P.E. with Mrs. Fatbeard.

"TODAY, WE WILL TAKE SOME FITNESS TESTS, ALRIGHT, ZUCCHINIS?" she screamed at us after Mrs. Firewood had dropped us off in the gym.

"Alright!" we all dauntlessly shouted back.

The first fitness test was doing 200 pushups a person, which everyone thought was frantic and simply impossible! Most of my classmates fell after only ten. Jeremy was doing pretty good until Brandon purposely knocked into him, so his score was only 20. Lilith's score was 98, but Mrs. Fatbeard still hadn't been impressed by anyone.

Then, it was my turn. Felicia, Ivan, Luxury, and I walked into the middle of the gym and got into pushup position. I balanced my tail in the air and waited for Mrs. Fatbeard to start the video that blared a voice that counted our pushups.

Suddenly, the voice shouted from her laptop, "BEGIN!"

I pushed up and down, remembering my number as the voice announced each number. Ivan fell after only two pushups, and he got up and told his score to Mrs. Fatbeard with a red face. Felicia tried to push Luxury over like Brandon did with Jeremy, but before she could, her hands slipped on the cold gym floor and she fell on her belly at only 10.

Luxury and I did the fitness test side by side until she wiped out at 19. Somehow, I managed to do 140 pushups until I fell. Everyone gawked at me in shock, and I felt proud of my muscular strength, which came mostly from being an Animalian. Mrs. Fatbeard explained that the next fitness test would mostly be about agility and flexibility. As soon as I heard that, I knew I could do well.

The first part of the test was the shimmy up and down a rope that was suspended from the gym ceiling. Next, we had to run to the opposite side of the gym, which had bowling pins scattered across it. We had to make it across without knocking down any of the pins.

Since I had done a good job in the first test, Mrs. Fatbeard told me to go first. I quickly scampered up the rope and down, and I deftly avoided all of the bowling pins and made it to the other side.

"Good job, pickle pie," said Mrs. Fatbeard as she plugged in my score on her computer. "NEXT UP, FELICIA CUTTER!"

Felicia confidently stepped toward the rope. However, she was wearing dress shoes today, instead of the recommended school uniform shoes. She had trouble climbing the rope and slipped many times. After her fifth try, Mrs. Fatbeard forced her to move on to the next activity.

Felicia held her skirt up at the ends like a dainty little princess as she skipped across the gym floor. However, her shiny pink shoes accidentally knocked over one of the pins, and her test ended there.

"Ugh," she whispered in Verda's ear from next to me as she took her seat. "My mom told me to never let Cat Freak show me down in everything. If I don't, she'll disown me..."

"Your mom's *so* harsh," Verda whispered back, but her eyes suddenly drifted to me, who was staring at them.

Her strikingly green and brown eyes narrowed slightly, and she cocked her head to the side at me. She smiled strangely and turned away. I was a bit flabbergasted at her strange gesture, but I bit my lower lip and turned away.

***

"Hey guys," I began to Jeremy and Lilith in the school garden during dismissal. "Want to go shopping at Humanian Goodies today? I heard they've had The Day of Spook costumes up for a while...and I was wondering if you guys wanted to check them out."

"Oh, that would be great!" exclaimed Lilith. "What time?"

"I'll go," said Jeremy.

"Maybe 3:30? Clara's babysitting me today since Mom and Dad have to go to a work party, and maybe she can take us?" I responded.

"Sure." Lilith smiled. "Humanian Goodies is on Fourth Wind Street, right?"

"Right!" I answered. I glanced at the bus loop a few feet away from us. Jeremy's and my bus had just pulled up. "See you then?"

"See you!" waved Lilith as we hurried to Bus #7.

***

When I came home at 2:30, Mom and Dad were upstairs, getting ready for their party. Clara told me not to disturb them, so I waited in the living room with my library book. 30 minutes later, the sound of soft feet coming down the stairs made me glance up. I held my breath as Mom, as beautiful as ever, walked downstairs with her beautiful blonde hair tied into a bun, a diamond necklace securely around her neck, and she was wearing a sparkling blue dress that brought out all of the tints and shades in her eyes. She smiled at me, and giggled, noticing that I was still holding my breath.

"Do you like it?" she asked, hugging me.

"You look amazing," I reassured her, breathing in her lavender scent.

She gently pulled away from me and pecked Clara on the cheek. "Be good to each other, alright? Clara, lock the doors. I assume you're staying in the house?"

"Actually," I interrupted. "My friends Lilith, Jeremy, and I wanted to go shopping today for The Day of Spook costumes at Humanian Goodies."

Mom frowned. "Oh, alright. Clara, you'll take them?"

A scowl spread across my sister's face. "But I wanted to relax at home for once and get to text my friends all day-"

I laughed at the mention of Clara's "friends".

Clara turned as red as a tomato, and steam seemed to be coming from her nostrils. "Shut up!" she hissed.

"Girls," chided Mom, but she was laughing too. "No fighting."

Dad entered the living room a few minutes later. He was looking quite handsome in his tuxedo, and his hair was slicked back from his horns. He held Mom's hand, and moments later, they left. Clara and I sat on the couch for a few minutes in silence, until she started chewing gum and turned on some icky teen television show called "Teen World". I glanced at the clock on the wall. It was only 3: 15. Humanian Goodies was only a walking two minutes away, so we still had time.

"OH. MY. GOSH!" Clara suddenly exclaimed, jumping up and down in her seat. "THE DRAMATIC PART CAME!"

I threw up inside. "Cool..."

Then, an idea popped up in my brain. I grabbed the densest, most large pillow from the couch, and hurled it at Clara's smiling face. The pillow landed squarely on her nose with a muffled *thud*, and the television remote in Clara's hand went flying.

"AGH!" Clara screamed, throwing the pillow off her face. "WHAT MAKES

YOU THINK IT'S OKAY TO DO THAT, PENELOPE?"

I laughed. "Technically, you."

Clara glared at me, then fetched the remote and rewinded the episode. It was 3:26 now, and I was ready to see my friends.

"Come on, Clara. It's time to go shopping."

Clara, at the sound of "shopping", immediately turned off the TV and sprang from her seat. "Yes! Don't expect me to pay for anything you nerds are going to get," she said maliciously. "I'm going to get a cool dress for the eighth grade dance."

"Wait, isn't that at the end of the year-"

"Hush," Clara said. "Come on, put on your shoes. We're going shopping!"

I nodded and quickly grabbed my black shoes with white outlines around it and my black jacket from the coat rack next to the front door. I was already wearing a nice black skirt and a white t-shirt.

"I'm ready! Let's go now, come on!" I shouted happily as I opened the door and stepped outside into the fresh air. Then, I hopped down the grass, past the fountain, and onto the sidewalk.

"Okay, okay wait up!" yelled Clara as she ran to me.

We slowly strolled down the quiet streets, heading towards Humanian Goodies. As we passed many shops and restaurants, I asked, "Hey, Clara, what are you going to be for The Day of Spook?"

I didn't know what she would say. Maybe something like, "I'm a teenager! Why would I ever wear silly costumes like you little punks?", but instead, she just looked at me. Then, she turned away and didn't say anything for a whole minute.

"I am thinking about being a white angel, if there is any in the shop,"

"Okay..." I said.

I didn't really think she matched character traits with an angel, but I didn't want to be rude. It was her choice, and I "kind of" respected it. Soon, I spotted Jeremy waiting outside of the shop, reading a seven thousand page book, and leaning on his bright green bike. I ran up to him.

"Jeremy!" I yelled to him, waving as I ran.

"Hello!" he said as he finally looked up from his book.

"Do you know where Lilith is? Is she late?" I asked as I ran up to his side.

Clara crossed the street up to Humanian Goodies, strutting up to us, flipping her hair like a rock star and trying to act cool as some boys her age walked past her. But suddenly, she tripped over a rock that was blocking her way, and she fell hard onto the hard ground close to the road.

"Clara!" I yelled, almost exasperatedly, but before I could run to her, I saw Lilith running up to her.

Lilith grabbed one of Clara's wings and hoisted her up before a Range Rover could turn her into a pancake. Clara seemed a little huffy after that. I guessed she was embarrassed that a "little punk" had saved her.

Lilith and Clara crossed the street over to us.

"Hey Lilith!" I hugged my friend. "Glad you came, and that you saved my sister."

I glanced at Clara. She pouted and stomped into the store, and we had to scramble in after her. When we opened the door, a little bell attached at the top dinged gently. Humanian Goodies wasn't the biggest department store around, but it had good stuff. We grabbed a few shopping baskets and set out to look for some good costumes.

"Ooh," I said, pointing to a new aisle, dedicated to the Day of Spook items. "Let's check that out."

Clara made a run for the women's section, leaving us alone in the aisle. We walked around, trying to spot any good costumes. Suddenly, Lilith found a cute witch costume that also had a little black cat stuffed animal that went along with it.

"Penelope, I could buy this, and maybe you could take the cat?" she suggested.

"Sure, I'd like to...but what costume would need a cat?" I asked.

"Well," Jeremy said. "You could always just dress up *as* a cat. It would be funny to see how the younger kids react, since some of them haven't learned about Animalians yet."

I frowned, but I tried to hide my slight disappointment. "Sure."

Lilith placed the witch costume in her shopping basket, and she helped Jeremy find the perfect costume for him. She grabbed a librarian costume and asked if Jeremy would like it, but he said he'd been a librarian, a zoologist, a kangaroo, the periodic table, and a mathematician already. The kangaroo seemed pretty random to me in the midst of all those other costumes, but I decided not to mention that.

"Hmm..." said Lilith, after Jeremy had told her all his past costumes. "How about this mad scientist? It has a cool wig and stuff."

Jeremy stared at the costume for a few moments. Then he nodded and placed it in his basket. Now, Lilith and I needed some special costume makeup. Lilith placed a face painting kit in her basket, so she could draw some mist and clouds on her face, she'd explained. I grabbed some fake whiskers since the ones I'd been born with couldn't be seen.

After we'd collected all the materials and accessories we wanted, we sped to the women's section to find Clara. We found her trying to decide between two identical-seeming red cocktail dresses.

"Um, Clara?" I asked, but she was too distracted looking between the two dresses, she didn't reply. "Clara...?"

Her head snapped up and she scowled at us. "What do you want?"

"We got what we needed. You have to pay for us."

"Nuh-uh," she shook her head. "Remember, I said that you punks have to pay for *your* things, *yourselves*."

"Please...?" I begged, trying to summon my best cat eyes.

"No."

"Please, please, please?"

"No!"

"Pretty please with a cherry on top?"

"NO!"

"PL-"

"NO IS NO!"

I frowned and stopped begging. "Alright, guys, let's go pay for *our* stuff. Clara's probably broke anyways." We began to walk towards the checkout.

Clara seemed to reconsider her choices as she checked her baby blue purse. "Wait!"

We turned around just as Clara came running up to us. "Please, punks, just this once! You were right…"

Jeremy smirked. "Alright, alright. Which dress are you going to choose?"

Clara looked at the identical dresses. "I can't choose between them. I'll just buy both and decide on the night of the dance-"

Having lost all patience, I grabbed the dress on the right from her hands and slammed it down at the checkout table. "We'll be taking this, and these things from the baskets, too."

The cashier glanced at Clara and me, a bit surprised at our traits. He tried to hide the shock on his face, but I could still tell how he truly felt.

"$50.99," said the cashier.

Jeremy reached into his pocket and took out a $100 bill. He kindly paid for all of our clothes and accessories, and we walked outside Humanian Goodies with stuffed shopping bags.

"See you on Monday," said Jeremy, as he parted ways from us. "I can't wait for Tuesday, the Day of Spook."

"See you!" Lilith and I waved.

Lilith high-fived me, and she walked slowly back to her own house too.

"What time is it?" I asked Clara as we walked towards home.

"Huh? Oh, it's like 4:43."

"When's Mom and Dad coming home?"

"Er...maybe eight?"

I frowned. "Aw, I wish they'd come sooner. I miss them."

We walked in silence for a few moments. Our house was only a few yards away, and for some reason, I didn't feel like talking anymore.

Suddenly, Clara did something unexpected. She placed a tentative hand around my waist, and she pulled me closer to her. I looked up at her face, surprised. She smiled warmly, which shocked me even more, since I hadn't seen her smile in that way in a long time.

She almost looked like Mom when she smiled like that. I was often told I had my mother's kind and sweet personality, and the same facial features as my father. However, Clara had her own special personality, and she looked a lot like Mom.

We walked up to our house, still in a half hug, but we broke apart as we set down our shopping bags in the living room and crashed on the couch. Since it was almost wintertime, the sun was pretty low in the sky, even though it hadn't yet set. Instead of putting on that dumb show "Teen World", she put on a funny family movie about a girl from another region starting school in a new town.

I felt like the director and writer had really done their job when portraying the main character's emotions. I could relate to how she felt in a lot of ways, and I understood how hard it was to leave everything you knew behind and start a new life. I squeezed closer to Clara, and we tilted our heads slightly together as we watched the emotional ending of the movie.

CHAPTER 13

The next Monday passed fairly quickly, and on Tuesday, Mrs. Firewood let us do some spooky-themed math problems for most of the day. I did really well on the order of operations pretest Mrs. Firewood had handed out, an "introduction" to order of operations, or even "what you already know about it" page.

I zipped through the pages, working diligently and correctly on each problem. Felicia had glanced over at my scratch paper where I had done the problems, and she grimaced at the way I worked out the questions.

"What type of solving method is that, Cat Freak?"

My face turned red. "I-I learned it in my hometown..."

Felicia burst out laughing and Verda snickered. I looked for Mrs. Firewood's support, but she had gone into the class across from us to ask about an upcoming project. *Take a deep breath, I* instructed myself. *Bullies only want a reaction out of you.*

I smiled at her. "Yeah, isn't it cool? I can show you how to do it sometime. Maybe your grade can improve from a D to a B?"

Now, Felicia's face was the one which was red from embarrassment and anger. "Hmph!" She turned away.

I realized that the whole class had been watching. Jeremy flashed me a grin and double thumbs-up. Lilith smiled, and Luxury pumped her fists in the air. I beamed at all of them. I was learning the way of life, here in Humania.

***

Finally, my bus arrived. Jeremy, Lilith, and I agreed to go trick-or-treating tonight in Jeremy's neighborhood, which was very large, even though Jeremy had warned us that the people were quite dull.

"The question is, do they have good candy?" asked Lilith.

"The dentist who lives across from us gives out toothbrushes-" Jeremy said, but then reconsidered his words. "I mean, some do, I guess."

Lilith and I nodded, and Jeremy dashed to the bus. I ran after him after saying "goodbye" to Lilith.

The bus was quite packed today. Thankfully, Brandon and his friends had stopped making fun of Animalians and spouting false knowledge about them. But, they had saved all of the seats on the bus with their backpacks, and I dared not ask them if they could move their bags.

I had to slide in beside a boy and a girl who looked very similar. They both had dark black hair and yellowish-green eyes, but the boy, who I was sitting closest to, looked uncomfortable as I slid in next to him. They both were probably third graders, so that meant they were younger than me, and hadn't learned about diversity. I tried to ignore the uneasiness the boy was letting out.

The twins got off at the first stop, which left me all alone in a seat. Somehow, I wasn't scared of buses, even after the disaster that everyone had gone through. And I wasn't quite as frightened by mountains as I used to be. For some reason, the difficulties we went through that day had strengthened me. I leaned my head against the window and closed my eyes. My stop was the seventh one, the second-to-last one, and I had plenty of time to rest a bit.

The bus abruptly stopped, and I could sense that it had stopped in my neighborhood. I dashed out of the bus and sped down the street before Brandon and his friends could catch me. Several times I thought they had come after me, and I felt silly every time I looked back to check.

When I arrived home, Mom was waiting for me on our white couch. "Hey, Penelope. How was school-"

"Good," I said hurriedly. "Can we go now?"

Mom raised an eyebrow. "Go where, exactly?"

"To Jeremy's neighborhood for trick-or-treating."

"Oh, right, you spoke of that yesterday. But, Penelope, no one's going to be trick-or-treating just yet. It's only 2:33."

I frowned and placed my backpack on the floor. "Ugh, I guess you're right. Is

Clara still being an angel? I heard you ordered a costume for her online."

"Yes, she is."

I nodded, and I ran upstairs to my room. I grabbed my laptop and logged in. I played a few online games for an hour, then read my new library book called Jumping Over by Shannon B. It was about a girl who faced struggles as she only had one arm, but she wanted to become a professional vaulter. I hadn't read more than a few chapters, but just seeing Shannon's familiar writing style made me want to read for hours and hours.

However, at 2:48, Clara burst through the front door. I was in the middle of a good part of my book, so I decided to greet my sister later. At least one hour and thirty minutes later, I ran downstairs and saw Clara attempting to do the splits on the carpet. She tried to stretch lower as her feet were already wide apart, but she ended up crying in pain and rolling on the ground like a roly-poly.

I laughed so hard my tummy hurt at this ridiculous scene. Clara noticed my presence and stuck her tongue out at me.

She rose to her feet and grabbed an apple from the kitchen.

"Hey Mom," I said, interrupting Mom's reports for work. "It's like 4:58. Is that a good enough time?"

Mom sighed and closed her laptop. "Alright, alright, go ahead. You guys can start putting on your costumes and get ready to drive over to Jeremy's."

As soon as Mom had said the sentence, I dashed up the stairs to my room and put on my fake whiskers and a black skirt and shirt.

When I ran back into the kitchen, Clara was begging Mom to let her go trick-or-treating with her friends Sakurai, Tony, and Lucia.

"Mom, please! I promise I'll be safe! Besides, Penelope and her friends are going to trick-or-treat by themselves, and I am literally older than them!" Clara complained.

"Alright, fine, I'll take you to Sakurai's neighborhood to trick-or-treat, but first I'll drop Penelope," Mom gave in.

I could sense that she had enough of Clara begging like a little kid.

"Thank you so, so, *so* much, Mom!" Clara yelled cheerfully.

I guess she didn't mind me being dropped off first, as long as she got what she wanted.

"Okay, then Clara, don't take too long to dress us! Mom said to hurry up, or we won't get to see our friends! I'm already ready, just waiting for you." I reminded her.

"Okay, okay!" yelled Clara as she rushed upstairs to put on her new angel costume.

Soon, she rushed downstairs with a plastic halo around her head and a pretty white flowing dress. Her long blonde hair was pulled into a braid that hung behind her back, and I had to admit, she looked like a real, heavenly angel.

"How do I look?" she asked Mom.

Mom smiled. "Amazing, Honey, I'm sure Tony will be impressed."

Clara turned several different shades of pink, and I snickered, but he shot me a glare. We left and locked the house, since Dad had the key. We unlocked the car and hopped in. Mom set Jeremy's address on the GPS, and we drove into the sunset towards his house.

***

When we arrived, a boy dressed in a strange wig and a scientist's lab coat greeted us in the driveway of Jeremy's house. I realized that it was Jeremy himself, and I hopped out of the car. Mom waved to me and blew me a kiss before she drove out of the neighborhood.

Jeremy and I were left alone in the driveway, and I realized that his big brick house had no decorations up. Mom had said we didn't need to go overboard with our decorations, but she allowed us to buy some pumpkins to place beside the fountain in our backyard. However, when I looked at the other houses in Jeremy's neighborhood, they all had amazing decor, but his house was the only completely bare one.

"So, is Lilith on her-" I asked, but before I could finish my sentence, I caught a glimpse of Lilith in her blue and white witch costume walking up to us.

"I'm here!" She came up to us and slipped her arms under ours. "Let's go, shall we?"

The sun had almost completely set by now, and some other trick-or-treaters had already started leaving their houses in groups. We trotted together, arm-in-arm, to the first house. It was the house across from Jeremy's, the place the dentist Jeremy had warned us about, lived in.

A man in a mask and white scrubs opened the door. He noticed that our trick-or-treating bags were empty, so he smirked and stuffed them completely with toothbrushes, toothpaste, and floss. When we finally managed to get away from the guy's house, Jeremy allowed us to throw away some of the hygiene tools he had given us.

"Well...we probably should have listened to your warnings," I remarked as we walked back down the driveway of the second house we had just gotten candy from.

"Yep," Jeremy grinned. "I told you so."

"Hey," I said, suddenly remembering something I had pocketed in my mind to speak about later but had forgotten about. "Jeremy, you said you wanted to tell us something back at the hospital. What was it?"

"Oh right," he said. "Remember that strange map Shannon B. had given us?"

"Yeah," Lilith and I said in unison.

"Well, I kept it with me all this time," he continued, reaching into his lab coat, and bringing out the map. "I think I know what each of the locations mean, and the symbol of the puddle."

"You do?" I asked in shock, even though I knew Jeremy could basically find out everything.

"Yeah...but I don't think this is a discussion to have out in pub-"

He was cut off by a group of little kids who complimented my cat costume.

"Wow," one of them said. "The tail is so realistic. I love your costume!"

"Thanks!" I smiled at them, even though I knew that the kids hadn't yet learned about Animalians. After the group had passed us, I turned back to my friends. "What were you saying?"

"We probably shouldn't talk about it in public. Come on, I know a place where we can talk."

CHAPTER 14

He led us reluctantly into the forest that lined the back of the neighborhood, and we stumbled through the dark and the thick weeds and branches.

Suddenly, we emerged out of the thick, onto a cliff. A few pretty fireflies hovered around, and I glanced down the cliff. A small, almost-completely dried stream of water trickled at least 30 feet below. Beautiful blue mountains were far in the distance, and as a cat, I wasn't afraid of heights, but Jeremy seemed a bit uneasy to approach the edge of the cliff. We sat down on the soft grass beneath us, placing our trick-or-treating bags down beside us.

Jeremy rolled out the map on the grass, and he pointed to each picture of the puddle. "So..." he began, "this puddle, I've read about it recently. I went through the public library last week, and I remembered that I had read a book about this strange, human-eating puddle before. So, I re-checked it out." He reached into his coat again and drew out a short library book. "It's not very long, but it matches up with the map. Apparently, this puddle was accidentally created in the Paradise of the Gods, up above, as a punishment for bad mortals. But somehow, it escaped from the skies and ended up on the earth. Legend says that it would travel from these six spots in Humania, sucking up any humans that would approach it. And you might ask, 'What if no one did?' Well, the pond somehow had a special magic to it that attracted any humans in the area."

"Really..." I said in disbelief.

Lilith sniffed in the silence beside me. She seemed to be in deep concentration, as if she was trying to remember something from her babyhood. A small thought in my mind made me wonder if this pond had a connection to Lilith's past, but I quickly ignored it.

"That's scary...There's a spot that's near a lake that's close to our school." I pointed to one of the puddle's stops.

Lilith glanced at it, and her eyes widened. "T-That's where my house is."

Jeremy and I stared at her in shock. "What?"

"H-How often does it travel between these places?" asked Lilith, still looking over the map.

"About every three years," said Jeremy.

"Three years?" I repeated. "But does it just stay in place for three years before it moves?"

"No," said Jeremy. "The puddle can resist the efforts the supreme powers are using to bring it back to the Paradise of the Gods when it is in those locations on the map. You see, after it's spent its fifteen minutes of just staying in place and luring a human in, the gods try to pull it back, so for the next three years, it's just hanging in between the Paradise of the Gods in the sky, and the ground."

"Oh," Lilith and I said at the same time. It was a bit confusing, but Jeremy seemed to understand it fine. "Interesting."

"But why did Shannon think this-" Before I could finish my sentence, the map began to glow strangely.

The puddle images shone like the sun, and the map flew up into the air, rolling into a scroll, and twirling. We all looked up in disbelief. The map suddenly flew back into Jeremy's coat. The fireflies suddenly swirled around us, and the sound of flapping from the forest startled me.

A huge book, about three yards long and two wide, pushed the trees aside as it emerged beside us on the cliff. I was stunned. It was a huge encyclopedia on the different types of trees, and it was opened in the middle.

It somehow was flapping, just by opening and closing its pages, just like a butterfly. The book seemed to have a mind of its own. It landed softly on the ground in front of us, and the glowing map in Jeremy's coat dragged him onto its spine. Lilith and I followed, very confused. We sat down on its spine, and the fireflies helped lift the book in the air.

We glided on the wind for a few moments, above Small Town. *This must be a book butterfly*, I realized, when I had regained my senses. Suddenly, the book faltered. I remembered that Jeremy had mentioned before that book butterflies needed some type of nature magic, specifically related to the air, to keep flying.

"Lilith!" I yelled. "It's a book butterfly! It won't be able to take us anywhere unless you use your magic to help it fly!"

Lilith nodded. Her hair suddenly turned a very light color at the ends, and her eyes became as pale as fog. The clouds, which were just a bit higher than we were at the moment, bent toward the book. It suddenly righted itself, and it glided smoothly. Suddenly, Lilith commanded the book to fly up through the clouds and above them.

I was mesmerized by the sight of the full moon. It was beautiful, and I couldn't tear my eyes away from it. My shortish hair blew out of my face in the light breeze, and my face shone like the stars. I suddenly felt like someone or something was staring at me. I glanced over at Jeremy, who was beside me. His face reddened when he realized I had caught him looking at me, and he quickly turned away. I raised my eyebrows, but I looked away as well.

Suddenly, the book butterfly, which I decided should be named "Piney", lowered slightly over a small house that was close to a sparkling lake that had a lot of fog over it. Beside the house was a field of many pink trees, but the kind, I could not tell from the height we were currently at. I immediately realized it was Lilith's home, but I was too stunned to say anything at the moment. The beauty of the whole experience was too much to take in.

When Lilith's hair returned to normal, I could see the map shining even more blinding than before. My eyes widened.

"What's going on? Is it showing us the location?" I asked in shock, determined to know what was going on.

"It's...working!" Lilith said, looking at the map in Jeremy's palms.

All of us, in amazement, looked at the map, wondering what adventures would be arriving like a breeze with this map as we sat on Piney, flying on the wind.

The Cat of Small Town

ABOUT THE AUTHORS

Ira Thackeray has been crafting stories since she was little. She has already published one book when she was six years old and is an aspiring movie director/author/zoologist/artist. She loves her family and always wants to bring out the best in others, and collaborating with her best friend Zeynep to bring this long-awaited story to life was very enjoyable. She is currently ten years old and lives with her family in the US.

Zeynep Sena Özkan is a 10 year old author who was born in Turkey and moved to United States when she was in third grade. She always had a passion for making stories and would write story ideas on papers or on the computer or on whatever she could find. Other than writing stories, she also loves to draw and read. She enjoys exploring nature, listening to music, and spending time with family and friends. Zeynep thinks that writing with her best friend, Ira Thackeray, and publishing her first ever book with her was an amazing experience.

The Cat of Small Town

CHARACTER KEY

Penelope

Lilith

Jeremy

Clara

Felicia

Brandon

Luxury

Mrs. Firewood

Shannon B.

Verda

Simona Rayband

Mrs. Wilder

The Cat of Small Town

MAP

The Cat of Small Town

PLACE KEY

Lith's Home

September Dawn Academy

Penelope's House

School Garden

Jeremy's House

Shannon B.'s Cottage

Made in the USA
Middletown, DE
07 April 2024